Wanda John-Kehewin handles complicated characters and tough situations with a clear-eyed sensitivity and grace. This story will wring out your heart, then hang it to dry in a sliver of sun.

—TANYA LLOYD KYI, author of *Me and Banksy*

If being able to hold two contrasting thoughts in your mind makes you a genius, Nevaeh is a genius. She sees who people really are—and who they want to be—and learns to open her heart to them no matter what. The pages of *Hopeless in Hope* end up being filled with the best kind of hope—hope that grows from a heart feeling full and right even when life pitches us around.

—ALISON ACHESON, author of *Dance Me to the End*

It's wonderful to read an author who so artfully channels the voice of youth. As Eva navigates serious challenges like living in a group home and being separated from her family, she observes the world around her, learning lessons about love, the ties of family and friendship, the unfairness of poverty, and the power of finding your voice. Oh, and also soup— the tremendous healing power of a bowl of homemade soup.

—JENNIFER MOSS, writer, podcaster, and creative writing instructor at the University of British Columbia

Hopeless in Hope

Hopeless in Hope

WANDA JOHN-KEHEWIN

HIGHWATER
PRESS

HighWater Press gratefully acknowledges the financial support of the Government of Canada and Canada Council for the Arts as well as the Province of Manitoba through the Department of Sport, Culture and Heritage and the Manitoba Book Publishing Tax Credit for our publishing activities.

Funded by the Government of Canada
Financé par le gouvernement du Canada | Canadä | Canada Council for the Arts   Conseil des arts du Canada

HighWater Press is an imprint of Portage & Main Press.
Printed and bound in Canada by Friesens
Design by Jennifer Lum
Cover art by Jason Lin

*With thanks to the graphic arts student focus group from the
MET Centre for Arts & Technology, Seven Oaks MET, and Maples MET
(Winnipeg, MB) for their thoughtful feedback on the cover of this book.*

Library and Archives Canada Cataloguing in Publication
Title: Hopeless in hope / Wanda John-Kehewin. Names: John-Kehewin, Wanda, 1971- author.
Identifiers: Canadiana (print) 20230166768 | Canadiana (ebook) 20230166784
ISBN 9781774920831 (softcover) | ISBN 9781774920855 (EPUB)
ISBN 9781774920848 (PDF)
Classification: LCC PS8619.O4455 H67 2023 | DDC C813/.6—dc23

26 25 24 23   1 2 3 4 5

ENVIRONMENTAL BENEFITS STATEMENT
Portage & Main Press saved the following resources by printing the pages of this book on chlorine free paper made with 100% post-consumer waste.

TREES	WATER	ENERGY	SOLID WASTE	GREENHOUSE GASES
52	4,100	22	180	22,700
FULLY GROWN	GALLONS	MILLION BTUs	POUNDS	POUNDS

Environmental impact estimates were made using the Environmental Paper Network Paper Calculator 4.0. For more information visit www.papercalculator.org

FSC
www.fsc.org
MIX
Paper from responsible sources
FSC® C016245

HIGHWATER PRESS
www.highwaterpress.com
Winnipeg, Manitoba
Treaty 1 Territory and homeland of the Métis Nation

To my children, Tan, Taylor, Kuna,
Kiyano, and Miya; my nieces and nephews, Aysha,
Chase, Salem, and Kineta; my brothers, Hank and Jay;
my sister, Bird; my late mother, Dorothy;
my late father, Herman; my grandchild, Kenley,
and future grandchildren.

May you all know the strength and resilience
of all the ancestors who lived before us.

1

A Quarter Can Ruin Your Life

COME IN OUT of the rain, my feet soaked and freezing in my leaky shoes. But I can forget almost everything bad in my life when I see my four-year-old brother, Marcus, and my nohkum. I look at Marcus's smiling face and I pick him up and twirl him around like he's as light as a pillow (and he almost is, but not quite).

Nohkum is standing at the stove, stirring soup in her gigantic pot. I call it her cauldron, but Nohkum's not a witch. She is magical, though. She can make a huge pot of soup that feeds all of us even when the fridge is empty.

Marcus giggles and shrieks as I spin him around. It's as if hearing him laugh makes all the bad feelings go away. It makes the world right again. We've been through so much together and we understand each other perfectly. Marcus is practically my life. He looks at me with his soft brown eyes and a hopeful grin. "Tickle game?" he asks.

I run into the living room and plunk him on the couch. I raise my hand in the air, bringing it down slowly, closer and closer to him. I know the anticipation is what makes him laugh the most. But this time, he stops laughing and starts coughing. He looks scared. I quickly pull him into a sitting position.

"What's wrong, Marcus?" I ask, louder than I expected to, my voice more like a shout.

He looks up at me and says in a whisper, "I swallowed my money."

"Swallowed your money?" I yell, then call out for Nohkum.

Nohkum comes running into the room, wiping her hands on her apron.

I tell her Marcus swallowed some money.

"Swallowed money?" she repeats and looks at Marcus, then back to me. "How much?" I shake my head and shrug my shoulders. Who even asks that in a situation like this? Nohkum does, that's who. She kneels down beside the couch and in a calm voice asks, "Marcus, did you swallow the quarter?" Marcus nods and big, fat tears roll down his face.

I pace back and forth, trying to push away the tightness in my chest, which is there like it always is. I have anxiety, or at least that's what Nohkum says, and from what I've read on the internet, she's right. My heart starts to beat too fast and my breathing comes in bursts.

Nohkum hurries back into the kitchen. I hear her dial the phone and tell the person on the other end that we need an ambulance. I don't know how she can be so calm. I'm freaking out because it's my fault Marcus swallowed the quarter. I'm angry at myself.

Marcus sits on the cast-off green couch Nohkum managed to get for thirty dollars. Before then, we had nothing to sit on but a few ready-to-go-to-the-dump armchairs.

"Marcus, why did you put money in your mouth?" I ask in an angry voice.

"I wanted to keep it safe. I wanted to buy us bubble gum," he whispers, and I feel my heart break. Here I am yelling at him when he was just trying to keep his money safe. What kind of person does that? Me, that's who. I am an ass. And not the donkey kind with a cute bow on its ear and an adorable sad face.

When Nohkum comes back in the living room, she asks Marcus if he can breathe and he whispers, "Sort of." She tells him not to talk anymore. She pulls me in for a hug and says everything is going to be all right. When she says it I believe her, because since she came to live with us, I've felt safe. Before that I was always worried something bad was going to happen to me and Marcus. But mostly Marcus, because he is too small to take care of himself.

I hear sirens wailing down our street before the ambulance arrives and Nohkum opens the door. Two paramedics come into the house with a stretcher. The cold creeps in as they stand there asking Nohkum questions. I see them scan the room and I feel ashamed. Through their eyes, I know it looks like poverty—and even smells like it, as the mildew seeps into the air from behind the walls.

We live in a hopeless old house on an almost-deserted dead-end street in a middle-of-nowhere town named Hope. This is the oldest part of Hope; eventually it will all be torn down and rebuilt into perfect homes for perfect people. Until then, we live here: imperfect people on an imperfect street that everyone forgets about. That's okay, because we pretty much want to be forgotten about anyway. Poverty isn't something to celebrate.

One of the paramedics calls Marcus "little buddy" and asks him if he can breathe okay. "I think so," he answers quietly. She tells him they are going to go for a ride to get some help taking the quarter out. Marcus whispers, "Will I get my money back?" The paramedics look like they're trying not to smile. Nohkum, who usually laughs at everything, doesn't find this funny. The paramedics gently place Marcus on the stretcher and buckle down his legs and chest. He reaches for my hand. "Eva," he whispers, his throat raspy.

"I'm here, Marcus, I'm here," I say, as I follow the stretcher down the rickety front steps. Out the corner of my eye, I see our cat running next door to avoid the commotion. I walk alongside the stretcher and stop at the back of the ambulance. I let go of Marcus's hand and he starts to cry.

Nohkum comes running out of the house carrying her purse, her usually neatly braided hair in a frizzy mess like one of those mad scientist wigs from the Halloween store. Normally I would laugh at her hair and offer to do it for her, but there's no time to worry about that now. She has taken off her apron and is trying to tame the wisps of salt-and-pepper hair sticking out in every direction. The paramedics tell Nohkum that Marcus needs to stop crying because the coin could shift and block his windpipe. One of the paramedics helps Nohkum climb into the ambulance and she takes Marcus's hand. He doesn't stop crying.

The dead grass and leaves are wet and cold under my feet. As the rain spits at the world, it's like all the warmth in my body gets sucked into the ground. Nohkum motions me over and asks me to tell Marcus to stop crying, because she knows he'll listen to me. He always listens to me. He says quietly, "Now I can't buy us bubble gum, Eva." The paramedic makes room for me and tells me and Nohkum to keep Marcus calm, then puts an oxygen mask over his face.

What would we do without Nohkum? I think to myself as I hold Marcus's hand and brush the hair off his sweaty forehead. The person who gave birth to us, Shirley, is nowhere to be found. That's the only thing we can count on from her— to not be there when we need her. She hates that I call her by her first name, but "Mom" doesn't seem right. I think that name has to be earned and she hasn't earned it—not by a long shot. Not sure if she ever will, but so far, she hasn't passed the test. I gave up on her long ago, back when she would let Marcus cry himself to sleep because she was drunk. Yes, I said it. Shirley is an alcoholic, and as the sirens howl and we speed off to the hospital, there's no sign of her anywhere.

2

Ugly Chairs, Bubble Gum, and Guilt

W HEN WE GET to the hospital, the paramedics whisk Marcus away and tell us to go to the waiting room. Nohkum and I sit side by side on the ugliest chairs I've ever seen. I don't even know why I notice. Now that the adrenaline is wearing off, I can feel sadness building inside me. I start to cry and Nohkum puts her arm around my shoulder, pulling me in and holding me tight. I trace the ugly pattern on the chairs with my finger, following it over and over.

Then I notice Nohkum's T-shirt and start to laugh. I can't help it. It says "SEXY" across the front in huge pink letters. Nohkum's always wearing T-shirts with slogans on them, usually something funny. Nohkum is sixty-five. I know she doesn't care if people think she's sexy.

Suddenly I remember where we are and my laugh turns into a sob.

"Eva, Marcus is gonna be okay. I promise." Nohkum looks directly at me, and I see the reflection of the fluorescent lights in her warm brown eyes. How can she promise that? I'm sure not everyone who goes into the hospital walks out alive. I know for a fact that way down in the basement there's a morgue, just like in the movies. But I trust Nohkum. I sigh and sit up straight. I'm crying. I'm laughing. I'm crying again.

"You know why I know everything is gonna be all right? Because the Creator has always taken care of me, and now the Creator will take care of Marcus." Nohkum places her soft, wrinkly hand under my chin and turns me toward her. Her face is like old leather. "You have to trust, my girl." I look into her eyes and nod.

Nurses and doctors and visitors walk back and forth down the long hallway, and I notice the wear and tear on the floor where thousands of people have walked before. I wonder if anyone else has noticed the tiles wearing away. Or is it just me being weird, wasting my time thinking about things that don't matter? It's helping me to avoid thinking that the worst might happen to Marcus.

"Do you believe me? Do you believe it will be okay?" Nohkum asks.

"I have to believe you," I say, "because how could I doubt a sixty-five-year-old who goes out in public wearing a shirt that says 'Sexy' on it?" I know it doesn't make sense, but it makes Nohkum laugh. It cuts through the tension. Nohkum pulls me close, and I feel her softness and warmth. I lean in and rest my head on her shoulder, her poky hair tickling my face. I try to tame it down, but it doesn't work. I pull the elastic out of my own hair and wrestle Nohkum's into a ponytail for her. She smiles at me. I want to smile back, to let her know I can be as brave as her, but I can't. I look back down at the floor.

I have trouble speaking around the lump in my throat, but I manage to say it anyway: "Nohkum, I don't know what I'd do without you." Wordlessly she pulls me close again, and I try to hold back sobs that want to escape, but somehow stay in, bubbling like the soup in her huge pot. "Nohkum? Promise you'll never leave me—I mean, us?"

"I can't promise you that, my girl, but I can promise that for as long as I'm here on this earth, I will always try my best. How about that?" I nod my head all bobbly-like, like I'm four years old, and she kisses my forehead and holds me tighter.

"He'll be okay. He has to be," she says, like she's giving an order to the universe. But she still looks a little worried.

The doctor comes into the waiting room just like in the movies and asks for the family of Marcus Brown, though he's already walking toward us, the only Natives there. Nohkum gets up and I see him look down and notice her shirt. It doesn't seem to faze him. Maybe his grandma has the same shirt. He tells us he needs a parent or caregiver to sign the paperwork because the only way to get the quarter out of Marcus's throat is surgery. Nohkum and I gasp at the same time, and I think we startle the doctor. He quickly tells us the surgery is non-invasive, which means there's no cutting, and it won't take long.

Nohkum still looks worried as she fills out the paperwork and signs it. Off goes the doctor. His scrubs must be new because I can hear a swish every time he takes a step. *Swish, swish,* like the waves at a beach I've always wanted to go to. Not like a beach at a lake, but the open ocean, where people actually surf. *Swish, swish, swish.*

WHEN WE SEE MARCUS after his surgery, he's sitting up in bed eating ice cream. He's groggy, but that doesn't stop him from gobbling up the hospital ice cream like it's straight from that expensive place with forty flavours. He offers me a spoonful. I tell him it's all for him. He tries again to pass me the spoon. I shake my head but Nohkum gives me a look, so I let Marcus put the ice cream in my mouth. Nohkum says you should always take whatever a child offers you because it comes from their heart.

Nohkum lowers one of the bed rails and sits next to Marcus. The window is covered with droplets of rain and the night has crept in. It looks lonely outside.

"My boy, never put money or anything but food in your mouth ever again, okay?" Nohkum says as she pulls her coin purse out of her pocket and hands it to Marcus. It looks really fancy and has tiny pink beads all over it in a flower pattern. I wonder who had all the time in the world to bead the entire surface of Nohkum's coin purse. Marcus opens it and pulls out a little plastic bag with a blackened quarter inside.

"That's the quarter they took from your throat," Nohkum says. Marcus tries to hand it to me.

"Ewww," I say, and Marcus laughs.

"We can still buy bubble gum, Eva!"

I look at my little brother. I love him for always trying to take care of me. It's a habit for us to protect each other. It started when Nohkum wasn't in the picture and Shirley wasn't really taking care of us. Just like now, when Shirley is who knows where.

When she comes home a few days later, we don't even bother to mention what happened. By then it's old news.

3

Hopeless in Hope

TRUDGING HOME FROM school in the rain with a hole in my shoe isn't my idea of fun. Nohkum tried to patch up the hole with duct tape and even tried to colour the duct tape black. But I took it off. I am not going to be caught dead with duct tape on the bottom of my shoe, even if it is coloured black. The glossy finish would surely alert the hostile crows in grade 9 who are attracted to shiny, unusual things. I know we're the poorest of the poor, but I don't want to announce what's already obvious. If I do get another pair of shoes, I know they'll already have been used by someone else anyway.

Nohkum tells me if she wins the lottery or at bingo, she'll take me shopping at a big mall in Vancouver and we'll buy everything we want, none of this secondhand shopping that we're used to. Nohkum also likes to say everything is new from the secondhand store—new to us. That's true, I guess, but for once I'd like to have shoes that no one's worn before.

When I get close to our house, instead of going inside, I crawl under the steps of the abandoned house next door to wait for the sounds of peace and quiet or the opposite: things being thrown or Shirley yelling at Nohkum. If it's quiet, it usually means Shirley has either gone out or passed out. I hope today will be a quiet day. The sky looks like it's falling, the way the clouds are layered, moving fast, a hint of orange-blossom sun peeking in from the west. I can see my breath. I rub my freezing hands together, watch our house, and wait.

Our old house is drafty in the winter and even draftier when Shirley doesn't pay the heating bill. That's when it's "colder than my ex-boyfriend's heart," according to Nohkum. It's funny to think about Nohkum dating. She definitely hasn't done that since she came to live with us.

Shirley says our house should have been torn down a long time ago. *But Shirley*, I think, *then where would we live? We, the imperfects? Where else would we have overgrown bushes and old appliances to hide behind when you're drunk and yelling at everyone and everything, even the cat?* The sounds coming out of our house when Shirley is drunk aren't really muffled by the bushes. Hiding is more of a comfort thing: if no one can see me, I don't exist. And if they can't see Shirley, she doesn't exist. If we don't exist, no one can point and laugh or feel sorry for us.

My real name is Nevaeh, which is "heaven" spelled backwards. I hate it. When people see it their tongues get twisted, a look of confusion settles on their faces, and they say it wrong, like it's a word from an alien language. It is

pronounced "Nuh-vay-ya." I came home from the hospital
without a name and was named a week after I was born. Who
doesn't name their child at the hospital? Shirley doesn't. She
says she was getting to know me and thinking of the perfect name. So, in the hospital I was Baby Girl Brown. I still
have the tiny hospital bracelet that proves it. Can't believe
my wrist was ever that small. Can't believe I had a pink card
above my vegetable-drawer-looking baby bed that read "Baby
Girl Brown." Lucky for me, Marcus couldn't say my name
when he learned to talk, so he started calling me "Eva," and
soon the rest of my family did too.

My nohkum says I'm lucky my mom didn't choose a
name like Lived. Get it? Lived spelled backwards? Not even
going to say it. Nohkum thinks this is the funniest joke ever.
She throws her head back and roars with laughter that comes
from a deep happy place inside her that Shirley, my mom,
her daughter, never gets to see. I laugh with her so she can
feel happy about making me laugh.

I don't think Nohkum has much to be happy about. Her
daughter is one of the town drunks who brings home shame
instead of food. Nohkum's never said it out loud, but I imagine that's what she's thinking. So, I try to help Nohkum as
much as I can and I laugh at her jokes, even when they aren't
funny. I know Marcus and I are the only reason Nohkum is
sticking around.

I have so much love for my nohkum and I tell her all the
time. She has a big, soft belly that's squishy and comforting
when she hugs me. Her favourite T-shirt says, "Bingo play-
ers make better lovers." The idea of Nohkum being a lover
grosses me out. She must have been, thirty-seven years ago,

because she had Shirley. But I prefer to think that she's like the Virgin Mary, only funnier and a better cook, who can make soup out of an empty fridge.

She is, I think, the only reason we have food to eat most days. Nohkum makes the most delicious soup and the softest bannock in the world. Shirley calls it "hangover soup" and goes back for seconds and thirds. It's a good thing Nohkum's soup pot is huge. She doesn't really have a recipe for the soup because it's made of anything and everything she can find. But no matter what goes in, the result is a whole pot full of soup brimming with smells that have seeped into the walls. I love the smell of our kitchen. It smells like Nohkum, so I guess Nohkum smells like delicious soup. Better than smelling like old stale beer. Better than smelling like Shirley.

Shirley walks around the house looking angry all the time, but I know when she goes out in the world she's not like that. I don't talk to her if I can help it. Nohkum doesn't agree with me not talking to Shirley, but she says she understands why I'm making that choice. One day, she says, I will talk to my mom. I just stare blankly ahead because I don't want to break Nohkum's heart by yelling "Not on your life!" at the top of my lungs.

My cat, Toofie, sidles up next to me in my hiding place under the steps and starts to purr. I found her in this exact spot two years ago. It seemed like no one really wanted her, either. She was shivering and cold and happened to be hiding from the rain at the same time I was hiding from Shirley. And so I brought her home.

She's a pretty smart cat. She knows to make herself scarce if Shirley is drunk. One of her ears looks like something took a bite out of it. She is white with brown and black spots and a tiny pink nose. Two of her paws are brown. The first time Nohkum saw her, she said something about her "two feet." Marcus asked if her name was Toofie, and that was it. I don't know which is worse: Toofie or Nevaeh.

Toofie and I wait in the rain, our tummies grumbling. I think about how I used to go to my friend Melody's after school sometimes and we'd have hot chocolate with cookies, homemade ones that her mom, Becka, baked. I can't imagine Shirley or Nohkum making homemade cookies. One time Nohkum made the ones that you slice from a tube. They were good, but not as good as Becka's. My mouth waters as I think about those cookies.

I haven't talked to Mel since the end of school last year. We became best friends in grade 5 when she moved to Hope, even though Mel's the opposite of me. She's tall and bubbly with the whitest, straightest smile I have ever seen. She could charm and disarm a person with her smile and her soft voice, so completely different from my gravelly voice. (I'd make a great short order cook, yelling out "Order up!") I asked her why she moved from Come By Chance, Newfoundland, to Hope, where nobody has a chance; she just laughed and called me crazy. (I looked it up! There actually is a place called Come By Chance.)

But we had a big fight about how I treat Shirley, how I avoid her and never call her "Mom." Mel couldn't handle that I'm not all mushy with Shirley, like she is with her mom. But Mel doesn't know what it's like to have a mom who's not like a mom at all—and she definitely doesn't know the whole truth about Shirley. She's never even been in our house, even

after all the years that we've been friends. That's something I
tried hard to avoid. And sharing the details of Shirley's end-
less screwups? No way.

Anyway, Mel had the nerve to call me selfish, well, to yell
it out actually, in front of everyone at school during lunch.
Maybe not everyone, I guess, but the other people eating outside at the picnic tables. Still, it was embarrassing. When I
told Nohkum, she said being a human on this earth is all about
life lessons. I don't know what the lesson is, though. I just
know that since our fight I eat a lot fewer homemade cookies and spend a lot more time at home with my m-o-t-h-e-r,
an alcoholic who doesn't give a crap about me.

With Toofie snuggled beside me, I pull my notebook out
of my backpack. I like getting all my thoughts down on paper.
It's one thing in my life that I can control.

WELFARE WEDNESDAY
Farewell Wednesday
The day she takes off
The day she decides it's okay
To leave her kids behind
Even when the cat has no kibble
And her daughter is counting on her.
Welfare Wednesday
The day she disappears
Like she has a job
And she's gone for normal reasons
Except she comes home super sick
Super sore, super poor
Super depressed.

The cat still has no food.
She hands me five bucks and says,
Get the cat a small bag.

This poem sucks and so does being poor.

4

Monkeys in the Bannock, Poetry in the Brain

WHY DOES IT have to rain so much? Even if I wear two of everything, I'm always cold. I hate being cold. What I really need is a new pair of shoes and a new jacket. I don't have a raincoat or even a warm coat— well, that's not exactly true: I do have a winter coat that once belonged to someone else. It looks like a men's jacket and has the logo of some company that probably went out of business a million years ago, maybe even in the seventies. Nohkum got it from the secondhand store last year and I thanked her for it. But I never wore it. I would rather wear two zip-up hoodies to school than an old man's jacket, so it hangs in the back of the closet, too big for anyone in our house but me.

Walking to school and walking home again in the cold, in the rain, is hard. There's a public transit system here but it's mainly to get to other towns and cities, like Agassiz or Chilliwack or even Vancouver. Getting anywhere in Hope on the bus is almost impossible. So I walk. Our house is a half-hour walk from the school, so I spend almost an hour a day walking. That's a lot of thinking time.

Even with all that thinking and walking, I am still overweight. "You're not overweight, my girl. You are pleasantly plump and not like those little stick boys and girls," Nohkum says. Nohkum is also pleasantly plump, but not as pleasantly plump as me. I think saying someone is "pleasantly plump" is a nice way of calling them fat. Shirley isn't fat at all. In fact, she is unpleasantly thin. I think it's her diet of cigarettes and alcohol. Who lives on cigarettes and alcohol? Shirley does.

One day, Marcus asked, "Why are you fat, Eva?" I wasn't mad at him; he didn't have hurtful intentions. I told him, "There's more of me to love," 'cause I want him to believe that. I wouldn't mind believing that too. He said, "I like how soft you and Nohkum are. Am I soft too?" I just told him we're like that because we love to eat bannock, and I wrote a poem about it for him.

BANNOCK AND MORE BANNOCK
(FOR MARCUS)
I am soft and fluffy
Like fresh bannock
Fried in grease
Hot, fat, and round
Bannock.

Bannock galore.
I want more!
Bannock and jam!
Bannock and ham!
Bannock and soup!
Bannock and sugar!
Bannock and cinnamon!
Bannock galore.
I love bannock.
Fluffy, round, and brown
Like me!

When I get to school, kids are milling around, smiling and laughing. Some have umbrellas, some have raincoats. Some of the girls are wearing WAMIS rainboots (pronounced "whammies"; the company's actually called Walk A Mile In my Shoes). I saw those boots at the mall when I went with Mel last spring and they cost over a hundred dollars. I'd never spend that much on a pair of rainboots—would never have that much to spend on a pair of rainboots—but they do look really good and come in lots of colours.

Mel is one of those people who doesn't like to wear name-brand clothing. She told me she doesn't want to support conglomerate corporations and child labour. I told her I agree that those things aren't good, and I do. But I think I'd still like to own a pair of WAMIS if I had the chance. All the girls at school are wearing black boots, but I'd choose purple.

I walk into the school. It's warmer inside than outside, but never warm enough to get the cold out of my bones. My first class is grade 9 English and we get to do a lot of writing.

We're studying all the different kinds of poetry out there. They all sound so foreign: sonnet, ballad, ghazal. It's not my kind of writing. I prefer free verse; it's like my thoughts flow straight onto the paper. Not that I want everyone to know my thoughts, which is why I never share in class when Mr. Perry asks us to. I think he's the only teacher who might understand poetry, pimples, and poverty, but I'm not interested in letting the other kids know how I feel.

There are a few kids that share in class, I guess because they think their writing is actually good. Some of it is and some of it is... not. But no matter how bad it is, Mr. Perry always thanks them for sharing. He treats us like our writing matters.

Today Mel shares a poem about her grandma dying. The love she had for her grandma shines in the poem. I wish we were still talking. I didn't even know her grandma died. Wouldn't a best friend know something like that? When Mel walks back to her chair, I see her face is red and I feel sad for her, but she doesn't make eye contact with me.

One boy reads the poem he wrote about waiting until grad to get his new car. I wasn't really interested in that poem, but the other kids laughed when he talked about never getting caught walking in the rain again or having to take the bus and sit next to a smelly kid. Of course, Mandy turns to whisper to her friend that I'm never on the bus so that's not a problem, just loud enough for me to hear.

Nohkum says to ignore mean people and they'll get bored and go away. I haven't seen that happen yet, because Mandy has been bothering me since she moved here from Vancouver in grade 4. What's the difference between kids in grade 3 and kids in grade 4? Nohkum once told me that kids are pure until they turn eight and after that they learn to lie. All of a sudden, they realize they can be mean and start figuring out ways to get away with it. I'm not sure how she knows this, but it sounds about right. I was so glad when Mel moved to the school in grade 5 because seeing her gave me something to look forward to, instead of just dreading the next mean thing Mandy would do or say. Plus, Mel wasn't afraid of telling Mandy to get lost.

When we were in grade 7, Mel made me cupcakes for my birthday. As Mel was carrying them to the front of the room, Mandy stuck out her foot and tripped her. Somehow Mel managed to drop to her knees but keep the tray of cupcakes from falling. She calmly got up, set the cupcakes on someone's desk, took one out, and walked over to Mandy. "I guess you'd prefer a squished cupcake, huh?" she said, and with that, she plopped a cupcake upside-down on Mandy's desk, smearing icing everywhere. Mandy was speechless, for once. It was pretty awesome.

The lunch bell rings, and Mr. Perry asks me to wait a minute. I know I'm not in trouble, so I'm curious why he wants to talk to me. Mandy looks back at me, staring and smirking. I have no idea how she can be so intimidating and mean in front of the teachers without them ever noticing.

I stand next to Mr. Perry's desk, still cold from the morning walk in the biting rain. He smiles at me and enthusiastically pulls a sheet of paper out of his briefcase. Mr. Perry does pretty much everything enthusiastically. "Nevaeh, *Medicine Wheel Magazine* is running a poetry contest. They want youth to write about what it means or feels like to be Indigenous. I've looked at last year's winning poems, and I know

this is something you have a really good chance of winning—
you're a great writer! Are you interested? If you'd like, I could
edit your poem for you. And first prize is a thousand dollars."

I take the flyer and stare at it. A thousand dollars is a lot of
money. First, I think I could actually get purple WAMIS, but
then I think I'd rather buy Nohkum a new bed and a heating
blanket for her arthritis. Some days it takes a long time for
Nohkum to get out of bed, especially when it rains. My mind
is racing. I thank Mr. Perry and leave the room.

As I walk away, I shake my head—like I could ever win a
poetry contest! I can't enter a poem about soup and bannock
or holes in my shoes or my drunken mom in a contest. But
that's what it's like to be me. What could I write that wouldn't
suck? *Thanks, Mr. Perry, for sticking more fluffy ideas in my
head!* I can't afford fluffy ideas. I can't even afford to buy lunch.

Oops, there go the monkeys in my brain again, having a
party I didn't invite them to. "Monkeys in the brain" is what
Nohkum calls it when I can't stop the negative thoughts that
go round and round in my head: *I am not good enough, I am
too fat, I am stupid, no one will ever love me, my own mother
doesn't love me, and I will never have a boyfriend because I'm
ugly.* I don't tell Nohkum all the things that go through my
mind because I think it would hurt her to know how I beat
myself up.

Nohkum says the monkeys jump from thought to thought
to thought, and I imagine a whole bunch of them in a big
room jumping all over their beds like trampolines. She says I
have to be kind to the monkeys and gently put them in their
cages. I imagine cages in the back of my brain, but they don't
have locks. The monkeys can come out anytime. But when

they start wreaking havoc in my head, they need to rest on their beds and give me a break.

I don't have anything to eat for lunch today, so I go to my usual spot under the stairs in the basement to wait out the lunch period. I carefully read the flyer Mr. Perry gave me. Second prize is three hundred dollars and third is one hundred and fifty. All the winners will be published in the magazine. But I couldn't win... could I? I think about what I could do with a thousand dollars, but... but... I shake my head and shove the flyer into the bottom of my backpack.

When the bell rings I head to my next class, which is gym. I hardly ever go because the PE teacher says if you don't have gym clothes then you shouldn't come to class. But Nohkum made me promise that I'd start going to all my classes, and I want to keep that promise. She tells me it will make her happy if I just try my best. It's a good thing she feels that way, because I am close to failing a couple of subjects. So today I'll go to gym. Why we have to run laps and sweat like pigs is beyond me, and why we need to do that to graduate makes no sense. How is throwing a basketball or serving a volleyball going to set me up for life? They should teach us how to do taxes, because I know that is one thing I'll have to do when I'm an adult. Nowhere on my resumé will I mention that I've scored one basket in my entire life.

When I walk into the gym, I see it's set up for basketball. Mandy is in her gym clothes—cute shorts and a matching T-shirt. Of course. I walk in and pile my stuff against the wall, and the teacher tells us to start running laps. Great! I hate laps even more than I hate Mandy. No, wait a minute, that's not true.

After the second lap, going into the third, I am huffing and puffing and my side hurts. I'm sweating and it's not the cute kind. Mandy, who is on her fourth or fifth lap, passes me and she doesn't even look tired. As she runs by, she whispers loudly (which is only possible for Mandy—I think it's her superpower), "Move it, fat ass." She says it so casually that I second-guess whether I've heard her right. But then I hear her friends laugh and I know she said it. I stop and put my hands on my knees and try to find my breath again. I can't even tell Mandy to fuck off because she's already on the other side of the gym.

After we finish our laps, the teacher splits us into teams. Of course, I'm opposite Mandy. I've never liked basketball, but I'll give it a good try for Nohkum. I promised. Promises are big to me and Nohkum: we promised never to lie to each other and we promised never to break a promise. I shouldn't have promised her, but I did. Making a promise in one moment isn't the same as living up to it in a different moment. But I can't back out now.

The game goes okay, since I just stay out of the way and try to shuffle my feet a little. Mandy is making baskets left and right. Her team wins and it's finally over. I gather up my stuff, feeling proud of myself because now I can tell Nohkum I went to gym class, and I even tried. She really wants me to pass high school and go to college. I want that too, but it doesn't seem real for me. I told Nohkum that after high school I'll get a job and help her and Marcus, and she got angry and declared that I *was* going to college. That's when she made me promise I'd try. So here I am, sweaty, out of breath, and a fat ass (according to Mandy).

I'm about to walk out the gym door when something hits me in the back of the head. I bring my hand up to my head, turn around, and see a basketball bouncing away from me. Mandy and two of her friends are pointing and laughing. What do I do? I run out the door, tears stinging my eyes. Mel's in the hall and I run past her and don't even look back to see her reaction. What if she's laughing too?

I walk home in the rain, which seems to be the only constant in my life. I am humiliated and angry, cold and hungry. I'm glad for the rain because it falls on my face and blends in with my tears. No one will know I am crying, not even Nohkum. It makes her sad when I cry so I try hard not to.

5

The Cat's Meow Soup

SIT AT THE old abandoned house and wait. I've pretty
much memorized the graffiti covering its rotting wooden
siding. The artwork is amazing and if I could draw anything but stick people, stick dogs, and stick pigs, I think I
could add something to it. If I could do graffiti, I could tag
Mandy's house and write something like "Mandy is a bitch"—
or even worse. As I think of all the things I could possibly
write, I wait and listen for sounds coming from my house.

Toofie appears from around the corner and rubs her soaking-
wet body against my legs. I pick her up and cuddle her to my
chest. She's shivering, so I slip her into my hoodie and zip it
up. Toofie seems to appreciate this; she purrs and stays still.
I listen closely but the house is quiet. I am relieved because
I won't have to deal with Shirley. I'm so hungry and I know
Nohkum will have food waiting for me.

I walk through the door and see Nohkum by the stove, wearing her Madonna "Crazy for You" Tour T-shirt. One day, many years ago, it might have been cool. Today it looks tired, but for some reason, it's totally Nohkum. I couldn't imagine her in a flowered blouse and a knee-length skirt like other grandmas.

I peek over Nohkum's shoulder into the pot. Today's soup has hamburger meat, onions, macaroni, carrots, corn, tomatoes, and a bunch of yummy spices she dashed in there according to no recipe in particular.

"My girl, do you know why this soup makes you feel better?" I already know why because she's told me many times, but I listen anyway. "I didn't only put hamburger and vegetables in this soup. I put my love and care into it. However you feel when you make something is how the person who eats it is going to feel."

I give her a hug. "Thanks, Nohkum. After a day like today I need something to make me feel better."

I sit down with a steaming bowl of soup, slather my bannock with fake butter, and dive in as if my life depends on it, 'cause it does. Fresh bannock dipped in soup is heavenly on a cold day like this, especially since I didn't have lunch.

Sitting here with Nohkum and listening to the soft scuff of her shoes against the broken, peeling linoleum floor makes me feel better. I know Marcus is napping because I see Nohkum's bedroom door is closed. Sometimes Nohkum naps with Marcus too, but not when she's making the soup that lasts for days. Nohkum says a well-made soup full of love can feed a whole town. I humour her because her pot is pretty big, but not big enough to feed a whole town. Her soup is magical, but miracles are different.

"Nohkum?" I ask.

"Mmmhmm."

"Why are girls so mean? Were they mean to you when you were my age?"

Nohkum thinks about it. "Why? What did they do?" she asks.

"Hit me with a basketball. It was Mandy who did it." I feel my face get hot just remembering how helpless I felt as I ran out of the gym, especially when I saw Mel watching the whole thing.

"Well, what did you say, my girl?"

I shift in my seat and break my bannock into pieces to soak up the rest of the soup. "I didn't say anything. I was all sweaty and embarrassed because Mandy and her friends were laughing."

Nohkum's eyes glaze over with sadness or anger, I'm not sure which—maybe both. "I can't believe the balls on some people."

"Mmmhmm." I nod and kind of smile at Nohkum using that word.

"What did you do?"

"I didn't really do anything. I just ran out and came home."

"I'll tell your mom to talk with that worker at the school."

"Nohkum, don't. Mandy will only do something worse next time. She's smart that way."

"I don't think that's very smart, throwing things at people," Nohkum says, scooping me another bowl of soup and buttering another bannock.

"Nohkum, if you tell Shirley, she won't do anything... she never does anything. She's too busy drinking. I just wish she didn't drink." I remember that Shirley tried to quit drinking once when Marcus was about two, but since then, nothing.

She used to go to these meetings, but after a few weeks she didn't bother to go back.

"I know, Eva. I wish she could take care of you kids so I wouldn't have to worry no more. She's working through some stuff, my girl." Nohkum stands behind me and gives me one of her warm jelly hugs.

"How long does it take to work through stuff? She's been drinking my whole life. What does she have to work through, Nohkum? If she had you for a mom, she should have been fine."

"My girl, you don't know the whole story. One day you will. Give your mom a break, okay?"

I know Nohkum wants me to say that I will, but I can't. I change the subject, which may be one of the only things I'm good at. "This is good soup, Nohkum, and the bannock is to die for!"

"I don't think anybody's ever died because my bannock's so good, but thank you." We both laugh. Nohkum's Madonna T-shirt has flour splatters all over it from frying the bannock.

"My girl, life is gonna be hard but you keep trying, that's all. Don't let what mean kids say or do bother you. See how old Nohkum is? I have been your age and believe me, you'll look back and see just how small that moment is. It's hard, I know, but believe me when I say you have every right to walk tall and proud."

"I know, Nohkum." I sigh and stop eating. "It's just hard. The kids at school, they know... they know Shirley's a drunk and it makes everything harder. I hate it."

"Things will get better, I promise. The Creator takes care of us." Nohkum pulls me to her midsection for a hug, and it is so soft and warm. "You know, my girl, depression runs in the family... your mom, my daughter, has depression. I have depression." I look up at Nohkum and she guides my stray hairs back behind my ears. "I hope you and Marcus don't get it, but it seems to run in the family. My mom had it too. You know they say depression can be genetic, so hopefully we can nip it in the butt."

I burst out laughing. "Nohkum, it's nip it in the bud, not butt! Why do people say 'nip it in the butt'? What would that even mean?" I roar with laughter and so does Nohkum.

Maybe Nohkum's right. What happened at school doesn't seem as big as it did earlier, especially now that I'm warming up and my stomach is full. Marcus walks into the room, rubbing his eyes, and I scoop him up onto my lap. Nohkum spoons him a bowl of soup. I nuzzle his neck and he tells me my nose is cold. I plop him down on his special chair, the one that's blue, and go upstairs to do my homework because Nohkum tells me to. I have to write a list poem for Mr. Perry's class with the title "Scary Things."

SCARY THINGS
Nohkum dying
Falling down the rickety stairs
Going to a funeral
Being on top of a mountain
Being on top of a building when it's windy
Having no food
Having no say
Having no Nohkum
Blood
Alcohol
Monkeys in the brain

6

Erase My Memory

WHEN I WAKE up, the sun is shining through the dirty window, creating grey shapes on the once-white wall. Now it's a yellowish brown from Shirley smoking in the house. She doesn't anymore, but she used to before Nohkum came.

It's Saturday and I don't want to be awake this early, but I have this feeling inside me, like my heart wants to jump out of my chest. Nohkum says she had that feeling when she was younger: it's anxiety. I asked her if it just went away, and she said it did when she stopped caring what people thought. Wouldn't it be nice not to care what other people think? As much as I hate Mandy, in a weird way I still care what she thinks about me. Crazy, huh?

The clock says 7:16 and my thoughts go round and round... and round. I can tell that the monkeys in my brain are starting to act up. All I can think is that I want to run away from everything: Shirley's drinking, Nohkum's sadness, Mandy's bullying. I want to call Mel and hear her voice telling me everything is going to be okay. I want to go back to sleep! But sleep runs away from me and my thoughts go to Shirley as I remember how she used to rock me to sleep after my dad left.

I didn't always hate Shirley. She wasn't always like a chicken with its head cut off. She used to read to me when I was little, before Marcus came along. It would be her and me cuddling just after it snowed and we'd be close together, warm and safe. She would sometimes buy us these awesome fries from a small mom-and-pop shop with the most delectable gravy. I'm not sure if I like the word *delectable*. Is it an old person word? Those fries were a treat though...

But I don't want to think about that. Just because you do a few good things doesn't make you a good person. I used to believe Shirley's lies and lap up her attention, but not anymore. It was just me then, but now there's Marcus, and he deserves so much more. He deserves a mom who will read him stories and give him baths and take care of him when he's sick. Instead, it's Nohkum who does all this. It's me and Nohkum.

When Marcus was little, but before Nohkum came, I missed school a lot because Shirley was either not home or passed out. Marcus couldn't look after himself, so I had to do it. One time I came home from school and Marcus had a full diaper and a rash had started, and Shirley was passed out on the couch. As soon as Marcus saw me, he ran to me, shaking. I let him soak in the bath for a bit and later I cried.

When I was younger and Shirley brought a man home, it was okay. I liked the attention. But one night when Marcus was little, he got sick and Shirley and her new friend acted like they didn't care at all. They turned up the music as Marcus cried in my arms with a fever. I think that was the night I stopped believing in her. I had been taken away from Shirley when I was younger, but I was little and I didn't understand. I'm not even sure how she got me back; it doesn't seem like she's changed much. Marcus wasn't taken from her because I took care of him.

Every single time Shirley brought someone home, we would hear noises coming from her room. I knew what the sounds were and I'm glad Marcus didn't. I got good at blocking them out by humming and singing to Marcus and focusing on his face. I would give Marcus his formula and he would drink it as he looked at me and tried to grab my nose. It was like a game to him and when he got bored, he would fall asleep. It melted my heart when Marcus felt safe enough to fall asleep. Shirley couldn't put him to sleep like I could. Since Nohkum came, Shirley doesn't bring anyone home anymore.

I don't have to miss so much school now either, and that makes Nohkum happy. She thinks I'll be the first person in our family to graduate high school. She says that with education you can free your mind and think for yourself. I want that. I want to be the boss of my own life. I want to help Nohkum and Marcus. One day Marcus and I will never have to see Shirley again. I'll make sure of that. I'll do whatever it takes to get us out on our own and we'll take Nohkum with us too. But until I figure it out, we're stuck with Shirley.

As much as I hate her sometimes, I still want her safe and I wait for her to come home. I'm always waiting and listening. Last night I didn't hear her come in, which means: (a) I was more tired than I thought and slept through her drunkenness, (b) she wasn't drunk and came in quietly like any normal mom would, or (c) she didn't come home at all. Why am I thinking about her when what I really wish is that she'd disappear?

My thoughts go round and round. Now it's 7:57. I'm never going to get back to sleep. I take a deep breath and picture the monkeys swinging back to their cages. The smell of pancakes drifts up from the kitchen. I hear Nohkum and Marcus giggling about something. When I head downstairs Marcus runs over to me. I pick him up and swing him around. I put my nose and lips on his face and inhale—he smells so sweet and his skin is so soft. Nohkum tells me to put him down so we can eat.

Nohkum goes upstairs to Shirley's room and I hear the door creak open. The morning quiet is broken when Shirley starts to yell. "Get the hell out of my room and keep it down! I'm trying to sleep! Just get out and shut the door!" So she did come home last night. All Nohkum wanted to do was ask her to eat with us, but Shirley can be malicious when she is hungover. Nohkum comes back carrying a beer can that she quickly tosses in the garbage and tries to cover with an empty flour bag.

Nohkum kisses the top of my head and we sit down to eat our pancakes. Expired pancake mix doesn't taste any different from not-expired mix. I love how Nohkum tries to scratch the expiry date off the box. Maybe it's because she thinks we won't eat it if we know it's old, or maybe it's because she doesn't want us to feel bad about ourselves.

Maybe it's both. I know that the food we eat comes from the food bank and a lot of it is expired, but I don't care. I admire Nohkum for standing in line at the food bank and not feeling ashamed. Me? Not so much. I'd die if Mandy or any of the other kids saw me standing in line for some day-old bread that Mandy's mom would have passed up on. But Nohkum tries so hard to make sure me and Marcus are never hungry.

I tell Nohkum I love her. Marcus joins in.

7

Wet, Stinky Shoes

T'S RAINING AGAIN as I walk home from school. The water droplets run down my face and my hair sticks to my forehead. My feet are soaking wet and no doubt my books are getting their share of rain through my leaky backpack. I approach my street and walk slower.

With Nohkum getting a pension cheque from the government and Shirley collecting social assistance, getting a new pair of shoes is kind of like winning the lottery. The odds are the same. Shirley's had a few jobs, but they never lasted. She'd be happy for a few weeks and talk about how great things were going to be. She would tell us that we were going to go shopping for new clothes or shoes or even a new TV so we could watch the shows that all the other kids were talking about. (If someone ever wanted to steal our current TV, good luck, you'd need at least three people to lift it.) My kid self would bask in her words, imagining I would soon be able to talk to the kids at school about the new vampire series that was all the rage, but do I really want to do that now? I think I'd rather talk with someone about how to survive life in Hopeless Hope than about good-looking blood-sucking teens with curfews.

Shirley was always getting fired or quitting her job because she was hungover or she was in one of her slumps where she couldn't get out of bed. Even though Nohkum says it's depression, it's hard for me not to see it as laziness. After time passed and we got none of the things Shirley promised, I stopped believing her, knowing her words were just like the ashes in her ashtray.

I stopped caring about how Shirley's lies affected me after a while, but I couldn't stop feeling angry when she lied to Nohkum and Marcus. They didn't deserve to be hurt by her. She told Nohkum that she would get her a new bed that would be better for her arthritis, because the one she was sleeping on hurt her back. She told Marcus she would buy him a new bike. I stopped believing her after about the thousandth lie and started to avoid looking at her when she talked to us. We were never going to get anything from her but mean words, empty promises, and embarrassing drunken episodes.

When I get to the abandoned house next door, I slide under the steps. Rain drips between the boards and falls onto my sweatpants. I watch the water droplets spread in darker grey ripples on my legs. I hear nothing coming from our house.

When I walk through the door, Nohkum is playing her country music softly and tapping her foot. The smell of soup and fresh-baked bannock fills the broken-down kitchen, making my mouth water. Nohkum helps me with my backpack and says, "Shhh, try to be quiet. Your mom is sleeping." I really don't know if anybody else's mother sleeps all day but mine is usually either sleeping off a hangover or still drunk and heading for one. I'm too hungry to care which side of drunk she is on. We have had soup three days in a row now but I'm not complaining, because three days of soup is better than no soup at all.

When I take my shoes off, my feet smell worse than the cat's litter box and my toes look like little light-brown raisins. "Pass me your stinky shoes," Nohkum says as she crumples up balls of newspaper. Nohkum stuffs the paper balls into my wet shoes to soak up the water, then hands me the baby powder.

Marcus pipes up, "Eva has stank shoes, Eva has stank shoes… so go, Eva, go! Boom boom!" He's busy colouring at the kitchen table, his dark hair falling across his cheek as he leans over the paper.

"That's a great picture, Marcus!" I say. "Can you tell me what it is?"

He looks at me like I am one chip short of a bag. "Eva, it's me and Daddy. There was no space to draw you, so you're somewhere over there." Marcus points to the living room and I know in his mind this makes sense. Nohkum and I look at each other knowingly.

My dad left when I was little, like Marcus's age, and Marcus's dad wasn't ever in the picture. I've tried asking Shirley about our dads but she doesn't answer. I know my dad was in jail, but I don't know if he still is. When I asked Nohkum, she said she never met our dads, but if she did, she'd shake their hands for having such beautiful kids. That doesn't tell me much, but I guess it's nice to hear.

I help Marcus pick up his crayons and I help Nohkum sweep the floor. Then I sit down, the moist warmth of the soup still in the air. It is another quiet day. Maybe quiet enough that I can focus on writing something for that poetry contest.

"Nohkum?" I say gently, because sometimes she gets so deep in her thoughts that I startle her if I talk too loudly. She told me before that it has something to do with residential school, getting lost in her thoughts and being scared like that. She turns down the radio and opens her eyes.

"Yes, my girl?"

I tell her about the contest and she tells me I can do whatever I set my mind to. She makes me promise I'll enter and I say that I will. I open my notebook and get a bit of soup grease on my paper. My impulse is to lick it off, so before I start to write, that's what I do.

I hate being cold
And hungry
And sad
Cuz mom cares more
About drinking
Than she does
For her kids.
I hate that
I think this way
And I hate that
It's true.

Yeah, right. Like I could ever submit that. I turn the page.

I live on the wrong side of town
On the wrong side of the river.
No one can find me deep in the
Heart of the hopeless in hope.
No blueberry bushes grow here
On the wrong side of town
And I question if the sky is more
Blue on the other side of town
Where the girls have cars
As soon as they turn sixteen
And they never have to worry about
Big noses, stretch marks, and being hungry.

8

Residential School, Depression, and Fart

SOMETIMES I THINK I might have a broken heart, but what does that really mean? I hear about broken hearts all the time. I imagine that my heart is nice and red but has fracture lines all over the place, like the old church Shirley tried to drag us to once.

Walking to school, I have too much time to think about what I don't have. I don't have a real mom, in the sense that I don't feel like Shirley really cares about me. I'm not even sure if Shirley and I have anything in common. I know she likes to write but I don't know what she likes to write about. Mr. Perry always talks about carefully choosing diction, so we say exactly what we mean. I wonder if Shirley carefully chose her diction when she wrote to my dad in jail. I once found an envelope with his name on it addressed to a correctional centre, but I haven't seen her write letters or get any mail from there in a long time. Maybe he got out or maybe he died. Either way, I've never heard from him.

Shirley has a purple journal, but I've only seen her write in it a few times. Nohkum gave it to her the first Christmas after she came to live with us. It's supposed to be a transformation journal, so it has prompts in it like "If I could change one thing it would be..." and "If I could go back in time, I would change..." and you're supposed to fill in the ending. It also has inspirational quotes in it like "One day at a time" and "Loving yourself is the best gift you can give yourself." I want one like it, but Nohkum doesn't have much money. I know she spends her pension cheque trying to keep a roof over our heads and our tummies full, which is more than I can say for Shirley.

Mel always hated it when I complained about Shirley. She said to me, "You are the angriest person I know. And you have no respect for your elders. What if you didn't have a mother?" And she didn't like it when I said I'd be just fine without Shirley as long as I had my nohkum. It's a lot to think about as I walk to school, looking at the earthworms trying to survive by coming up to the surface in the middle of the busy sidewalk.

Just as I get to school, it starts to rain. Again. For now, I'm thankful I didn't have to slosh around in the puddles with my crappy shoes, even though I'll have to on the walk home.

In social studies, Mr. Harris asks if anyone has ever heard of residential schools. A few kids raise their hands. *Of course, I've heard of a freaking residential school*, I think, but

I don't dare say it out loud. Nohkum went and so did my grandpa and that's where they met. Nohkum says the teachers kept them apart, but they used to pass notes to each other through other students. Nohkum also says that the residential school was a scary, terrible place to be. That's when she got depression, after going to residential school.

When I read about it, I think maybe I have depression too, but I'm still trying to figure it out. Depression isn't tangible but it feels tangible to the person suffering from it. According to the dictionary definition of "tangible," things you can touch are tangible. I guess food is tangible and hunger is intangible. So depending on the time of the month, Marcus and I are either tangible or intangible—ha! Bad joke, I know.

Mr. Harris is looking at me and the kids are laughing. *Oh shit!* I missed something. My focus comes back to class. "Um. Could you repeat the question, please?"

"I asked if you knew anything about residential schools." Mr. Harris stuffs his hand in his corduroy pants pocket.

"Um, yes, I know about them," I stutter, to more laughter from the beasts in grade 9.

"Do you mind sharing with us?"

"Um, I don't know. My nohkum went there and she said it was awful. I don't know much else." I squirm in my seat and feel my face turn red. My freaking ears are burning. I want to sink into the floor.

Then someone lets out a fart and I am the first to laugh. *Oh my god!* My laugh echoes in the small classroom and then I think, *Oh geezus, what if they think it's me?* But Mr. Harris says, "Thank you for sharing, Nevaeh, and whoever else shared with the class."

The boy who farted pipes up. "Thank you, thank you very much!" The class erupts in more laughter and I am off the hook... for now. I join in the laughter and, if only for a split second, I feel like I am a part of something.

Mr. Harris goes into detail about some of the things that happened at residential schools, the physical, sexual, emotional, and even spiritual abuse, and talks about how we can do better and be more understanding by learning about history and other cultures. Mr. Harris tells us there were 139 residential schools in Canada and the last one closed in 1996. I don't even know which residential school Nohkum went to. Mr. Harris talks about the Truth and Reconciliation Commission and tells us to look at the Calls to Action for homework.

I remember Shirley saying that when she was in school, the other kids teased her and called her a "savage." I asked her what she did about it, and she said, "Nothing. I can't fight against the whole country." My thoughts wander back to class just as Mr. Harris dismisses us for lunch. My sense of belonging doesn't last because the fart is forgotten and no one is laughing about it anymore.

Today, I've got a lunch that Nohkum packed for me. I open the paper bag: a peanut butter and jam sandwich on fresh store-bought bread, oatmeal cookies, and a bottle of orange pop. Nohkum got her cheque last Friday and bought Marcus and me all the food we like.

I am starving and finish it all. When I get home, I'll tell Nohkum what Mr. Harris said about residential schools and about the interrupting fart. I know she'll laugh and her belly will shake and I will laugh with her. She'll try to cover her toothless smile like she always does—but if she's wearing her false teeth, I'll secretly hope they fall out like they sometimes do and we'll laugh even harder!

9

No Nohkum, No Soup

TODAY HAS BEEN one of those days that isn't so bad, I think, as I leave school in the pouring rain. I know I could borrow Nohkum's umbrella, but she got it at one of those free places and it has big, ugly flowers all over it. I wish I could be like Nohkum and not care what other people think but—oooh, there goes Mandy in her family's perfect minivan and it looks like even their damn dog is perfect because it's wearing a pink raincoat. Oh my god, wait 'til I tell Nohkum that Mandy and her dog have matching raincoats!

I don't wait at the house next door before I go inside. I'm in a good mood and I know that whatever happens, Nohkum will be there. I walk into the house and it's quiet. Too quiet. There's no soup on the stove. I open the door to Nohkum's room and she's not there. But where is Marcus? I run upstairs to his room but it's empty too. Where is everyone? I even check Shirley's room. She's not there either. Marcus and Nohkum are always here. I am worried now.

I sit on our green hand-me-down couch, noticing the brown patches of someone else's dirt. I twist my hands together and feel my heart start to beat fast. I tell myself to breathe. I tell myself maybe they went for a walk or to the store. But Nohkum and Marcus are always here when I get home. The monkeys in my brain start having a free-for-all, trashing their beds and cages and jumping from one horrible thought to another.

I hear footsteps on the front porch and run to open the door. It's Shirley, with a sleeping Marcus in her arms.

"Where's Nohkum?" I practically shout. Marcus stirs and turns to look at me.

"She's in the hospital," Shirley says calmly, like she's telling me Nohkum went shopping.

"What? What happened?" I can feel a huge knot forming in my stomach and I can't breathe.

Shirley looks at me for a few seconds before she answers. "She broke her hip. She slipped on the front steps."

I can feel tears in my eyes, but I don't want Shirley to see them. "I need to go see her! I thought you were going to tell the landlord to fix the steps!"

"The doctor said no visitors today because they're trying to get her pain managed."

I don't know what to say, so I don't say anything. I take Marcus from Shirley and sit on the couch. Shirley goes up to her room. The silence is lonely. Tears start to fall down my cheeks. Marcus looks at me and asks, "Why are you crying,

Eva?" He traces the path of a tear with his index finger. He watches me for a minute, then says, "I'm hungry."

I make us some no-name macaroni and cheese and give most of it to Marcus.

What am I going to do? I think to myself, and the fear is real because I know that Shirley won't take care of us and my mind races a million miles too fast and I muffle a sob. Marcus gobbles his mac and cheese and asks for juice.

Shirley comes downstairs, looking like she's been crying. She gets a drink of water and goes back upstairs. Marcus and I sit on the couch with the TV on and I rock him back and forth until he falls asleep in my arms, just like he used to.

The door to Shirley's room squeaks open again and I hear her make a few false starts before she appears in front of us.

"Eva, I know you don't want to hear from me, but we're going to have to work together now that Nohkum's in the hospital. I should have kept after the landlord to fix things around here, then maybe she wouldn't be in the hospital right now." She looks unsure of her words and her actions and finally she decides to go back to her room. For once, she does not slam her door. It feels like any jarring noise right now will break our family apart even more.

I leave Marcus on the couch and go to my room. I lie on my bed for a long time, thinking. I think about Nohkum. I think about Shirley and drinking and Marcus and me and how I should work on my poem for the contest instead of letting the monkeys jump around in my head—but how can I focus on writing a poem if bad things keep happening? I don't even want to enter the stupid contest... but I have to because I promised. I promised Nohkum. But... sometimes promises can be broken—right?

10

Things That Break

DON'T GO TO school the next day. Instead I peek in on Shirley and tell her Marcus is still sleeping and I am going to the hospital. She nods and her eyes are all puffy. I almost feel sorry for her—then my other smarter self says that whatever pain she is feeling right now is exactly what she deserves. Then the self that Nohkum brings out in me does feel sorry for her and I tell her to have a good day. Shirley nods again.

At the nurses' station, I ask where Elsie Brown is and they tell me to follow the blue line on the floor to the geriatrics ward. I go to room 27C and see Nohkum lying in one of the beds, her toes peeking out from under the crisp white sheets. I have to hold back tears because Nohkum is part of my put-together world. I don't even trust Shirley with Toofie. It's always Nohkum who makes sure Toofie has food, even if it's from the food bank. Imagine that: the food bank even gives out cat food. It isn't always the same brand, but Toofie is happy with anything.

I stand at the foot of Nohkum's bed and I'm not sure what to do. A tear rolls down my face and suddenly Nohkum yells, "Boo!" I am so startled I step back and grab my chest. Nohkum laughs, or at least tries to laugh, and I can tell she's in pain. She reaches for me and I gladly go into her arms. I feel like I am home when I'm in them. I start to cry harder. Nohkum says, "Don't cry, my girl."

"Nohkum, are you coming home soon?" I rest my weight on the bed and bury my face in her chest and Nohkum flinches from pain.

"I don't know, my girl... I don't know yet."

I am quiet for a minute to gather my thoughts. "I'm scared," I say quietly, my voice breaking.

Nohkum looks sad. "Why? I'll be home as soon as I can."

"What if Shirley drinks and drinks and leaves Marcus alone or I can't go to school or we don't have food or Marcus gets sick or..." My sobs permeate the air.

"Shhh, Eva. I've talked to your mom and asked her not to drink for a while."

"But Nohkum, Shirley always drinks. How is she gonna stop drinking?"

"Try and believe in her, my girl. Please stop crying. You have to be strong for Marcus, for your mom, even for Toofie. Your mom promised me that she would not drink while I'm in here."

I cry until there are no more tears. The nurse comes in and says I shouldn't be putting any pressure on Nohkum or the bed because Nohkum needs to heal. I get up and sit on a chair that at least a million people have sat on before me.

Just like our pukey green couch at home, except these chairs are diarrhea yellow.

"Nohkum, do you want anything to drink?"

"No, my girl, this medicine they give me makes me so sleepy. I need to rest."

I nod and she closes her eyes.

I already miss seeing Nohkum in her funny T-shirts. She looks so frail, wearing a hospital gown that someone probably died in... ewww, what a morbid thought.

The nurse says it's time for Nohkum to have more pain medication. Nohkum takes the pills, then drifts back into sleep. She starts to snore softly and I know I'm even going to miss her snoring.

Before she leaves the room, the nurse tells me Nohkum will heal fast because she has a feisty spirit and that gives me some hope.

I walk home and stop at the house next door but I'm not listening for sounds. My heart hurts too much and I'm embarrassed to show Shirley how sad and lost I feel. Toofie comes up to me and I grab her and cry hard into her fur. I am afraid because life before Nohkum was scary. When I stop crying, I pull out my notebook and write a list poem. Will this be the poem I enter into the contest? I don't know. I can never be sure of anything...

THINGS THAT BREAK

Vases full of dead flowers thrown at your absent mother

Noodles from the dollar store where your family shops for food

Pencils from the dollar store where your family shops for supplies

Plastic toys from the dollar store where your family shops for birthdays

Holey holy shoes that splish splash splosh on the way to effin' school

The promises that your mother made over and over to quit drinking

Your grandmother's hip and it's all downhill from here

Hearts of kids that arrive in care thinking their mom doesn't love them...

That's me at five. I will always be five.

11

Nothing's Funny Now

THE NEXT DAY, I feel like I've been hit by a Mack truck. That's something Nohkum says when she's sick. When I get to school, my mind is racing and my heart is sad. Mandy picks the worst time to say something to me.

"Where did you get the ugly coat? It looks like something from the sixties that my grandpa threw away!" I hear laughter start right next to her and travel through the crowd toward me.

Today I'm wearing the coat I never wear, the old man's jacket that Nohkum got for me. When I woke up this morning I was freezing and sad, and I thought about how Nohkum believes in taking care of the body first and if it looks good, great, and if not, who cares? I wanted to try not to care like she tells me to. But it hurts that someone would say something about the coat Nohkum picked out for me. It's too much.

"What the fuck is your problem, Mandy? You're such a bitch!" As I turn to face her, Nohkum's advice to not worry about what other people say flies out the window. I am seething. The smug look on Mandy's face? I just want to slap it off. I know Nohkum would say violence is not the answer.

"Oooh, she's got a voice that sounds like the sixties too! Whatcha gonna do about it?" Her hands rest on her hips like Nohkum's do when she's mad at Shirley.

"Get the fuck off my way, bitch!" I say as I push past her.

"You'll be sorry you ever did that, trash!" Mandy yells to my back.

I am too tired to respond. I go to social studies and Mr. Harris is still talking about residential schools. I don't even half listen, and instead just doodle in my notebook. I write my name, Nohkum's name, and Marcus's name over and over in different styles. I like the bubble letters best and I'm busy colouring them in when I hear someone saying my name in an upset tone.

"Nevaeh!" I see Mr. Harris standing in front of me with his hands on his hips and I wonder why everyone is putting their hands on their hips today. Pretty ironic, because the person it reminds me of has broken her hip.

"What the hell do you want?" It slips out before I can even think about what I'm saying.

"Neveah, you need to go to the office. Now!" Mr. Harris points to the door. I shrug my shoulders and feel everyone's eyes on me, but my face doesn't turn red. I am too mad; instead, I see red.

I don't go to Mrs. Thompson's office. In fact, I walk right by it without even slowing down. For some reason, I'm not afraid of getting in trouble. I walk out the front doors of the school.

I turn toward the hospital and keep walking. It's raining, of course, and I left my ugly coat in my locker, but at this point I don't care.

The nurse at the nurses' station tells me Nohkum is sleeping and I can only stay for a few minutes. I don't even answer her. I just walk to Nohkum's room and sit in the ugly yellow chair next to her bed and cry silently. I have no one to talk to about what incredible bitches everyone is.

Nohkum moves in her sleep and groans a bit but doesn't wake up. I look at her face and study its familiar wrinkles. I wish she would wake up and listen to me and tell me what to do next.

I hear someone clearing their throat behind me and turn around quickly. There's a tall woman standing in the doorway. She has a hospital ID hanging around her neck.

"Hi, my name is Miranda. I'm a social worker here at the hospital." I turn back toward Nohkum and try to wipe my tears without Miranda seeing me. "You must be Eva," she says in a soft voice.

"Yeah," I say, figuring Nohkum must have told her my name.

"Do you mind if I come in and sit down?"

I shrug. "It's not my hospital, so I guess you can sit anywhere you like." There is silence as we both watch Nohkum sleep.

"Your Nohkum told me you two are really close," she says. I nod.

"She also told me that she worries about you and your brother." I wipe another tear off my face with my grubby sleeve. "Eva, is there anything I can do for you?" I look at her for a second and she looks like she actually cares.

"Naw," I say, and get up to leave the room. Miranda stops me.

"If you ever need anything or want to know how your Nohkum is, just give me a call. This is my personal cell number." I take the card she's holding out to me and stuff it in my back pocket.

As I turn away, I hear one of the other patients in Nohkum's room fart, and for the first time, it isn't funny. I walk off, hands in my pockets and eyes on the floor. Farts are supposed to be funny. But not this time. Nothing is funny now.

WHEN I GET HOME, soaking wet, Shirley has a sandwich waiting for me. "I made you grilled cheese, Eva. Probably not as good as Nohkum's but it tastes okay, right baby?" she says as she tousles Marcus's hair.

"I don't see how anyone can mess up grilled cheese." I see a moment of hurt pass across her face and feel sorry until I see how quickly it turns into a hardened glare.

"Eva, I'm trying, I really am."

We've had one of those weeks where it is so quiet and tense that you're just waiting for the other shoe to drop, or as Nohkum says, waiting for the cat to realize its tail is on fire.

It's been an entire week and Shirley hasn't had a drink. I still don't trust that this is for real. I keep expecting her to slip up. I'm just waiting, 'cause when she does I'm going to have to be "mom." The longest Shirley's ever gone without a drink is probably about three months. I hope she can do it again, or at least hold on until Nohkum comes home.

I sit down and dig in because I didn't have lunch today and I'm starving. Marcus says hi and starts swinging his leg back and forth, kicking the table leg. Usually this doesn't bug me, but today I snap at him to stop. He looks at me, hurt in his eyes. I jump off my chair, give him a big hug, and tell him I'm sorry.

Shirley has her back to me as she over-scrubs at the chips in the paint on the green ceramic stove. A green ceramic stove, like I've seen in old magazines from the fifties. Nohkum has a magazine from 1952 and the recipes in it are horrendous. One casserole recipe calls for canned peas and cream of mushroom soup. Ewww, no, and ewww, gross.

"Eva, I need you to watch Marcus on Friday morning." Shirley looks tentatively at me, then quickly back at the stove and adds, "If you can."

Marcus is distracted by his grilled cheese. I clear my throat. "Why? I have school."

She turns to face me. "I know. I shouldn't ask but... I have a job interview."

I sigh. "Why are you looking for a job now? Who would watch Marcus while you're at work?" I know I'm not being nice, but I can't help it.

Shirley looks flustered. "Well, there's daycare subsidies and... oh, why am I explaining to you? You're a kid!" She throws the sponge in the sink, then storms up the stairs to her room and slams the door.

Marcus reaches for his milk. "Mama's mad?"

I nod. "A little bit. But not at you, okay?"

Marcus eyes the half sandwich on my plate and I give it to him. I walk up the stairs and stand outside Shirley's room. I knock softly on the door and not too loud, but loud enough she can hear me, I say, "I'll watch him Friday."

12

WFA
(World Falls Apart)

WHEN I GET home after school, there are two cars parked in front of our house. One is a police car. I walk in and see Shirley sitting on the couch with Marcus on her lap. There's a lady dressed like she's going to a funeral and a cop standing over Shirley. There's a man in dark clothes standing off to the side. I hear the word "removal." I stand between Marcus and the lady, who I know is a social worker. I know it. I know it in the way she stands and the way she holds some sort of file on a clipboard, and how she looks down at Shirley as Shirley stares holes into the threadbare carpet. Why can't she look at me?

I have to do something. "You guys can all leave now. I can take care of my brother until my grandmother comes home,"

I announce with fake confidence. But when the social worker asks, "When do you expect her back?" I don't have any words. For some reason, Shirley pipes up: "My mom broke her hip and she's in the hospital. She won't be back home for at least a month." I wish she'd shut up. The social worker looks at me like she's studying me—and she probably is.

She smiles at me, a big smile, and says her name is Mrs. Chester. I don't think this is the same social worker who took me when I was little, almost ten years ago. This one is too young, but she's already practised smiling while taking kids away. She makes me think of the Cheshire Cat from *Alice in Wonderland*, her name and the look on her face. Shirley and I watched that movie together once and the Cheshire Cat's smile freaked me out. It could smile even if it was dying... or at least it seemed that way when I was little. That movie scared me so much I still won't watch it. Like, who falls down a secret hole and wants to go exploring? Not me, that's for sure.

Mrs. Chester, the Cheshire Cat, acts like she owns the place and our lives. And at this point, she does. I ask her why she's removing us and she tells me Marcus tried to walk to the zoo and was found four kilometres from here. An elderly lady stopped him and called the cops. I wonder how he managed to cross the road on his own. Why was he going to the zoo? And where was Shirley when this was happening?

The Cheshire Cat says when the police phoned the house, there was no answer, and when they got here, Shirley was passed out. I look at Shirley, expecting her to deny it. But she doesn't. She just sits there and tears start to roll down her face.

The homewrecking social worker takes Marcus from Shirley. I jump forward, but the cop steps between us. Still, the

Cheshire Cat doesn't stop smiling and I notice that her teeth
are a bit crooked. "Nevaeh, please don't make this harder
than it has to be. Honestly, things will go better for everyone
if you just co-operate." I want to strangle her! How's that for
co-operate? She writes something on her clipboard.

Shirley keeps staring at the carpet and I hear her gulp
just once. That gulp sounds exactly like she just took a sip of
beer. I stare at her and I know I look mean. I stare at her so
hard she can feel it and she looks up and I see what looks like
fear in her eyes. How can she be afraid of me? I'm only a kid.
Sometimes I feel like I'm fourteen going on thirty-seven, and
she is thirty-seven going on fourteen—but I'm still the kid.

Marcus starts to cry and tries to pull away from the
Cheshire Cat. "Eva! I don't wanna go! Don't let them take
me!" What am I supposed to do? There's only one thing I
can do—I start to cry too.

"Marcus, everything's going to be okay, I promise!" Marcus is crying and breathing in big gulps of air. It reminds me of
something I read, about Breatharians, who think they can live
without food or water. Who thinks about Breatharians when
their brother is being taken away? Me, I guess. That's who.

"Eva!" Marcus's howls split the air and I can't hear the
loud buzz of the fridge anymore. He reaches for me and I
step toward him, but the cop puts his hand on my shoulder
to stop me. I read somewhere that police can only put their
hands on you if they're arresting you. I turn to face him and
shove his hand away. "Are you arresting me?" He shakes his
head and I'm confused. This is all happening so fast but it
feels like slow motion, like time has frozen. I've heard about
people's lives falling apart and now it's happening to me. It's
unreal and yet so real.

Shirley stands up and walks out of the living room. Just like that. Nohkum says I'm not supposed to let the hate I feel for her multiply, but I can't help it. I stare at her back as she walks away.

Marcus throws himself on the floor and the Cheshire Cat has trouble pulling him toward the door. I can tell she is used to taking away screaming kids. She clears her throat and lets go of Marcus for a second, then adjusts her perfectly coiffed hair and her purse strap. She motions for the other social worker standing at the door to help her with my screaming brother. I start to make a run toward Marcus, but the cop holds me from behind. I try to throw my head back into his face but end up bumping it uselessly against his chest.

I can't be helpless! I use my right foot to kick the cop's leg from behind and I hear him grunt. He holds me tighter but doesn't say a word. Marcus is carried away by the social workers, down the rickety steps, yelling my name. He isn't screaming "Mom," he's screaming "Eva." I sink to the floor and the cop stumbles forward. He probably wasn't expecting me to fall apart as soon as my brother was out of sight.

I cry deep sobs that come from a place inside me I didn't know existed. This is the worst thing that's ever happened to me and Nohkum isn't here to fix it. My heart feels like it's squeezing tighter and tighter and I swear I am going to have a heart attack. It feels so tight, like it might break apart at any moment. I remember last summer when Nohkum taught me how to braid sweetgrass. She made me do it over and over again until the braid was tight enough. My heart feels like a really tight braid that's about to come undone. Blades of sweetgrass everywhere, except where they're supposed to be.

The Cheshire Cat comes back into the room. In a nasal tone she says, "Okay, Nevaeh, your turn. We have a placement for you overnight in a group home." A group home? As much as I hate my poor excuse for a mom right now, I would rather be here with her.

"Why can't I just stay here?" I ask in a whiny voice. I hate myself for not being strong enough to say that I'm not going, no matter what she says. It's what I mean to say, but it doesn't come out that way.

The cop stands nearby but doesn't touch me again. The Cheshire Cat comes toward me. "I'm sorry, Nevaeh, there is no other way. You have been legally removed." She speaks gently, peering at me through her glasses. I wish she was rude, so I could yell at her.

I feel my body shake and my voice shakes with it. "Why are we being removed?"

She sighs and her smile disappears. "As I said, your brother was found four kilometres away, walking on his own, and when we called here, there was no answer. Do you know how lucky he is that nothing bad happened to him?" I do know this, and I sort of nod while trying to wipe away my tears. "When the police brought Marcus home, they found your mother on the couch passed out from drinking alcohol. Do you see how dangerous this is? Your mother has a problem and you children aren't safe here." I know she's right, but it doesn't make me like her.

I look at her with her high heels, perfect hair, and expensive purse. I know if I could just rewind time and stay home this morning, Marcus would be with me instead of being taken away by this person who doesn't even know him. But

I know I don't have a choice—I've been through this before and these strangers are going to decide what happens next. This is happening to Marcus now, just like it happened to me when I was little. I wish Nohkum was here but she isn't. It's just me and I've let them take my brother! *Oh, Nohkum! I don't know what to do!* A fresh wave of pain, anger, and shame washes over me. It's like I can actually taste it when I breathe in. Even the air has changed. It smells empty.

"Now come on, Nevaeh. Go pack whatever you need for tonight and your school bag. We need to get going." I nod and tell her and the cop I need a few minutes alone in my room to get my stuff. They tell me they'll wait for me at the front door. I hear them talking and laughing quietly about something other than our lives being ruined. I close my bedroom door gently and look around. Everything looks like it usually does, only now nothing is the same.

I take my books out of my backpack and throw them on the floor. I grab some socks and underwear, a pair of sweatpants, and a few shirts and stuff them in the bag.

And I do it. I quietly unlock the latch and open the window slowly, hoping it doesn't creak, and I climb out. I land in a puddle and the puddle sloshes. Toofie is waiting below. I pick her up in my arms and run next door and we hide under the steps where we first met. I hold her close and cry into her fur. I hear them calling my name.

I fall asleep with Toofie tucked into my hoodie. When I wake up, it's dark and still raining. The only consistent thing in my life is the rain. Toofie struggles out of my sweater and I let her go. Then it's just me under the steps, rain falling through the cracks and onto my head. I'm cold but I don't care. Marcus crying for me, his small face as he's being dragged away, is all I see. I get up, walk to the front window of our house, and look in. I see Shirley lying on the couch, her best friend, beer, sitting on the coffee table beside her.

It's so hard to trust someone when they don't give you any reason to. Why did I think things could be different? After the first time I went into care, it took me years to stop watching for social workers' cars, even when I was walking to school. For some reason, social workers' cars always look like old police cars. Is that the look they're going for? Big, scary cars they can fill with lots of kids in one fell swoop? That's what the social worker's car looked like the first time I was taken away... when I wished I had a sister or brother to go with me because at least we'd have each other.

I rack my brain and try to figure out what to do next. I can't go to the hospital, not until the morning. I think about Melody, who I haven't spoken to in months, and with the rain soaking my soul, I decide to at least try.

13

Not Real Bannock

ELODY'S MOM, BECKA, answers the door and I am too tired to even try to think up an explanation for why I'm there. She looks at me for what seems like hours but is probably only a few seconds, then opens the door wider. I step inside and start to cry. Becka helps me take off my wet hoodie and puts her arm around me. She leads me into the living room where their dog, Daya, sits on the couch wagging her tail. Daya inches closer to me and lays her head on my lap as I tell Becka what happened. I cry the entire time.

Mel walks in the door calling for Daya, then sees me sitting there, with swollen eyes and snot running down the hollow above my lip. I quickly wipe it away. Mel just stares, and I can't read her face. Did I used to be able to read her face? It's only been four months since we stopped talking, but it seems like such a long time. Becka excuses herself and takes Mel down the hall. I hear them whispering.

When Mel and Becka come back into the room, Becka's carrying a blanket, sheet, and pillow. Mel stays standing, but Becka sits next to me and pushes the hair in my face behind my ear. I usually don't like anyone touching me, especially my hair, but I don't say anything. Mel clears her throat. "My mom says you can stay 'til tomorrow morning and we can figure out the rest then." She uses a soft voice I almost don't recognize. I think I see pity in her eyes and that is not what I want. I want her to say, "Come sleep in my room," like she used to, but she's looking at me like I'm a bird with a broken wing and I don't enjoy the feeling it leaves in my empty stomach.

My tummy lets out a loud growl. "You must be hungry. I'll make you something to eat. Come help me, Mel," Becka says. Mel and Becka leave the room again and I am alone with my thoughts. I keep seeing Marcus's face and I am lonely and I am angry. I told him nothing would ever happen to him while I was around. He's never going to believe me again. This thought starts a fresh wave of tears and muffled sobs and I feel like I'm never going to stop crying. My shoulders hurt. Why do my shoulders hurt? I sob into the pillow and see it's a Starscape Man pillow and that makes me cry harder. Starscape Man is Marcus's favourite superhero. Marcus likes him because he glows like a bright star when he's helping people. Marcus has always wanted a Starscape Man blanket set but we could never afford it. Maybe Shirley could have—should have—used the money she's spent on drinking to buy it for him.

Becka comes in carrying a steaming bowl on a plate with bannock on the side. I reach for the plate and my arm shakes under its weight. The bowl is full of chicken noodle soup from a can and I can tell the bannock isn't fresh—it's got to be at least a few days old. It tastes nothing like Nohkum's. I don't say anything. I tear off pieces of bannock and let them float in the soup until they're soft. The lump in my throat gets bigger as I think of Nohkum's soup and bannock and her lying in the hospital looking small and pale. I'd never seen her look so small.

Becka sits beside me again and Mel takes a seat on a chair in the corner. She looks uncomfortable. We sit silently, watching the TV. It's some show I've never seen before, with a loud laugh track. No one moves to change the channel. It all feels a little surreal—maybe a lot surreal. It's weird how in someone else's house the same sounds feel totally different from when you hear them at home. I want to wake up from this stupid nightmare, but it just keeps on going.

After I finish eating, Becka stands up. "Well, it's time for bed, Mel. Nevaeh, you can make up your bed on the couch. Things will look better in the morning, okay?" I nod.

Mel calls for Daya as she leaves the room but Daya doesn't go with her. Becka tells Mel to leave the dog with me. "Animals are intuitive about this kind of thing. Nevaeh needs someone right now." Daya puts her head back on my lap.

After a few minutes, the house is quiet. I look at the clock ticking on the wall and it is 9:45. I take my notebook out of my backpack and, flipping through the pages, see the half-written poems, one-liners, and other words that will never see the light of day. I turn to a new page and start writing.

Alcohol calls to you
Like your children never could
And you answer its call
With sure steps and gulps
Like you can trust what it does to you
When you can't even remember us
While I sit in the corner
Wondering why you had children
Our stomachs grumbling from hunger and hatred
Breatharianism by force of someone else's will.
Yours.

14

Nowhere to Run

'M JOLTED AWAKE by a heavy knock on the door. The clock says 7:30. I hear someone walk down the hall and unlock the door. Then I hear the Cheshire Cat's voice loud and clear. "Good morning, thanks for calling us. Is she still here?"

I get up quickly, but I know there's no point in running. My heart starts to beat faster and I can hear it in my ears. I can't breathe, or maybe I've forgotten how. Can you forget how to breathe?

The Cheshire Cat walks into the living room. She smiles and says, "Good morning, Nevaeh." What an awful thing to say: my world has been ripped apart and she expects me to have a good morning—and she's the one who took Marcus! What right does she have to talk to me and pretend this morning is just like any other morning?

Becka steps toward me. "Nevaeh, honey, I'm sorry. It's illegal to harbour a runaway, to have you here and not tell anyone. I had to call." She looks upset, but I glare at her and fold my arms. I realize Daya is gone. Another traitor.

"Nevaeh, I'm taking you to a group home. Do you have everything you need? If not, we can always pick some things up." I tell them I need to use the washroom and they nod. They start talking to each other as soon as I leave the room. I lock the bathroom door behind me. There's no way I can fit through this window. I run the water to give myself some time to think. But I have no way out. I turn off the water and slowly open the door. The Cheshire Cat is there waiting.

As we leave, Becka calls after me, "Nevaeh, it will get better, I promise." I don't bother to look back or answer. I see Mel out the corner of my eye wearing a huge cardigan that must belong to her mom. I'm not sure why I even notice what she's wearing. She looks like she's been crying.

The sun is coming up, but it is still cold. The Cheshire Cat opens the back door of the big, boxy car and I slide in. This car seems exactly like the one I rode in the first time I was taken from Shirley: cold and impersonal, with no hint that kids have ever been in it. No crunchy old fries, no toys from sad meals, no traces of children left behind—or maybe any sign of them has been wiped clean. Essences of the surreal. The Cheshire Cat shuts the door behind me and I am slammed back into the present moment.

She gets in, starts the car, and drives. She looks at me in the rearview mirror, her blue eyes staring at me from behind blue-rimmed glasses. "Nevaeh, I know you're angry and scared and you don't trust anyone right now." She refocuses on the road. I say nothing and hug my backpack closer. She continues. "I know the lady at the place we're going and she's super nice and super helpful." I still don't say a word.

"Her name is Grace. There are other kids your age there and regular meals, and even a foosball table." A foosball table? Get real here—it sounds like a retirement home. And she says "regular meals" like we never ate properly at home. Nohkum always made sure we ate regular meals! How dare she assume that would solve all my problems, like I would be happy away from my family if someone just gave me regular meals! She continues to try to fill the silence with words that don't mean anything to me.

"Your brother is in a good home too." My ears perk up. The Cheshire Cat looks in the mirror again and sees that now I'm actually listening. "He wasn't crying when we dropped him off. I stayed with him for a little while and we played a game. He asked for you and I told him he would be seeing you and your mom very soon." I am trying not to cry. I do not want her to see me cry. When they know your weakness, they can use it against you. Marcus is my weakness. And my strength.

She continues to drive, turning here, turning there, until I don't recognize where I am anymore. "Nevaeh, you have every right to be mad and sad, I want you to know that. I was in care too when I was a child." I know she expects me to respond but I can't. I am not usually rude to people; when I am, it's because they have done something wrong.

We pull into the driveway of a big house. It doesn't look like I thought a group home would. It looks like a home. I expected it to be square and have bars on the windows.

Instead, it has a nice lawn and flowers in the garden. The door opens and a woman appears and motions for us to come in.

We walk up the steps and the woman puts her hand on my shoulder and guides me through the front door. She makes eye contact with me. "Hi Nevaeh, I'm Grace. I'm so happy to meet you." She reminds me of Nohkum.

I nod and trip over my own feet, dropping my backpack on the floor. "Now that's what I call making an entrance," Grace says through a smile and I have no choice but to laugh, just a little.

The Cheshire Cat laughs too but I glare at her and she stops and clears her throat. "So. I'll be bringing by the paperwork for you to sign next week," she says to Grace. "She hasn't brought much so let me know if she needs anything else and I'll arrange to get it for her."

Grace rubs my back and I sort of flinch like a puppy who doesn't trust anyone. "I think we'll go shopping together and I can just get the receipts to you." Grace turns to me and asks, "Nevaeh, would you like to go shopping with me?"

I'm surprised that an adult is speaking to me with respect—at least I think it's respect. I hope it's not pity. I nod and Grace smiles at me.

"Nevaeh, I'll be by next week to see how you're doing," the Cheshire Cat says. "I've already called the school and let them know the situation so you don't have to explain anything. The school counsellor knows you may need someone to talk to." I keep my back turned to her and I don't respond. "Well... I've got lots of work to do, so I'll leave you to get settled in."

Grace nods. "We'll see you next week, Mrs. Chester." I can't imagine the Cheshire Cat being married, let alone

having kids. She dresses funny, her glasses don't match her
face, she has crooked teeth, and she smells like old potpourri.

Grace leads me to a bedroom with bunk beds. It's a light
purple colour that I think is called lilac. I've never worn anything lilac, and nothing is lilac in our house, but it's a pretty
colour. She tells me I'll be sharing the room with Misty. "You
can have the top bunk. Misty's already settled on the bottom. One thing I must mention is that Misty is non-binary,
so please refer to Misty as *they* and *them*. Do you know what
'non-binary' means?"

I nod. "It means you don't identify as male or female."

Grace smiles. "You'll meet them soon when they come
home for lunch. You can use the bottom two drawers for your
things. Everyone here knows your space is your space. They
aren't allowed to go into your things and vice versa, but I'm
sure you already know that.

"Curfew is eight o'clock on school nights and nine o'clock
on the weekend, but for the first week you need to come
home right after school.

"On weekdays, breakfast is at seven and after you eat, you
can pack your own lunch for school. Dinner is always at five-
thirty but breakfast on the weekends is served at nine. If you
want to eat earlier, you can grab cereal or toast.

"We have weekly assigned chores here. Since it's your first
week, you won't have to participate, but I'll add your name
to the list for next week. We also have meetings on Fridays,
so there's one tonight. You came at a good time. Do you have
any questions so far? I know there's a lot to take in." I shake
my head and start to feel nauseous. "Well then, I'll let you
put your stuff away and I'll be back in ten minutes to give

you a tour of the rest of the house. How does that sound?" I
nod and Grace leaves the room.

This room feels so empty. No pictures on the walls, and
no mess on the floor. I miss Nohkum and Marcus. When
will I see them again? I unpack my bag and definitely don't
need two drawers. I sit down on the bottom bunk and wait
for Grace to come back.

She taps on the half-open door and asks if I'm ready. I
get up and think, *No, I'm not ready*, but I follow her anyway.

We walk down the hall, and she shows me where the
bathrooms and other bedrooms are. One is hers. She tells
me there are three other youth besides me and Misty living
here right now. I'll meet them tonight.

Grace walks into a smaller room with two computers.
"This room is for homework and using the internet. But you
have to earn time and show you're responsible enough to
limit your usage. Everyone has one hour of free time a day—
there's a sign-up sheet by each computer. Homework comes
first though, so if someone needs the computer to do homework and you're just using the internet, homework trumps
free time."

There are so many rules and I'm not sure if I can remember them all. It's like Grace reads my mind: she tells me
she'll give me a sheet with all the rules and guidelines of
the house on it, and I'll have to sign it to say I'll follow them.

We go into the kitchen and there are locks on all the cab-
inets. Grace tells me to sit down and makes me a turkey and
lettuce sandwich. She tells me all the knives are locked up
so if I need one, I have to ask permission and sign it out.
Things have sounded okay to this point, but now it sounds

like prison. Why are the knives locked up? It's like she reads my mind again. "Some of the kids can't have access to sharp objects, so even scissors need to be signed out." I wonder what kinds of kids live here.

A kid with a cool haircut shaved up to the crown on one side and longer on the other side walks in like they're carrying the weight of the world (and they might be).

"Misty, say hello to our new resident, Nevaeh," Grace says, and is completely ignored. A minute passes before they glance over at Grace and take out an earbud.

"What?"

Grace repeats herself.

"Oh. Are they going into the room at the end of the hall?" Grace shakes her head.

"They're with me?" Misty says with a look on their face that leaves me feeling scared. Is this who Grace keeps the knives away from? For some reason, I pipe up. "I don't mind sleeping by myself so she can have her own room," I say to be helpful, in a voice I don't think I've ever used before. But as soon as it comes out, I know I've made a mistake.

Grace notices right away. "Misty's pronouns are 'they' and 'them,' Nevaeh," she says gently. "I'm sure you'll remember from now on."

Misty grabs a banana off the counter and a diet soda from the fridge. "I'm not interested in sharing my space, Grace," they say, looking at me, and storm out.

"Don't worry about Misty—their bark is worse than their bite," Grace says. "And I think it will be good for you to share a room. It might be nice for you both to have some company."

I nod, but not because I agree. I just don't know what else to do or say.

15

Cabbage Rolls and Baggage

WALK AROUND THE empty house, empty of laughter, empty of the voices you'd expect to hear. I hear nothing but the sounds of silence and water swishing rhythmically in the washing machine. In the living room, there is a fireplace with a mantel. A mantel like you see in books, except this one doesn't hold photos of the family that lives here. I imagine hundreds of kids have been through these doors. The light-purple room, my room, has a big window that faces a yard. The yard has a tree with a tire swing hanging from it. Not that I'd ever go on the swing, because how embarrassing would it be if I broke the branch and landed on my butt?

The afternoon passes slowly. I stay in my room, listening as the other kids come home from school, until Grace calls me for dinner. It smells amazing. I take a seat, but I keep my head down as the kids gather to fill their plates with cabbage rolls and rice. Nohkum made cabbage rolls once, but they weren't as big as the ones Grace has piled high on the serving platter.

"Take more," Grace says. "Otherwise the masses come like locusts and there'll be nothing left for you." I reach for another cabbage roll. Grace puts her fork down. "You've all noticed that we have someone new joining us tonight. This is Nevaeh."

The others introduce themselves. There's a boy named Jared with hair styled to one side that I think looks cool, another guy named Ty with long hair tied in a bun, and a girl whose name is Rhys. She's a little on the bigger side, like me. Misty doesn't say anything, just keeps their eyes on me.

Jared pipes up. "Mmmm. Grace, did you put lemon in the rice today?" Grace nods and I bring a forkful of rice to my nose and breathe in the buttery lemon smell. I would have thought it would smell like laundry soap or something, but it smells delicious. I want to enjoy my food, but I feel self-conscious about wolfing it down. I miss my mouth anyway and drop some rice on my pants. I pretend it didn't happen, even though I think Jared saw me trying to secretively sweep the rice off my sweatpants. Everyone else ignores me and I like it that way. I wish it wasn't so awkward. I would trade miserable Shirley for this awkwardness with these strangers any day.

After dinner, Grace tells us to meet in the rec room in half an hour for our Friday night meeting. Misty and Jared do the dishes and I sit at the table twiddling my thumbs, as Nohkum would say. I hear Misty whisper something about me not doing chores because it's my first week, then laugh as if it's a great joke. I don't see what's so funny. My first impression of Misty is that they like to exclude people. If Nohkum was here, she'd probably be able to tell me why. She'd say something like, "Hurt people, hurt people." Maybe Misty wants to push other people away before they're the one that gets left out. I don't know them well enough to have it figured out yet.

I'm the first one into the rec room, followed by Grace. She gives me what I think is a warm smile, but really, what adult can I trust besides Nohkum? She's the only one who's never lied, to me or anyone else. There are posters and pictures on the off-white walls. One of the posters has a quote from Rumi: "As you start to walk on the way, the way appears." I think about what it means and I like it.

Misty and Jared walk in and sit backwards on their chairs, and I think about how I've only seen people do that in movies. Rhys and Ty walk in together. We are all seated now and as I sneak a peek at Misty, who is chewing their nails, I notice Ty picking at a pimple that sits right in the middle of his forehead. I tell myself not to shake hands with him, or at least to make sure he washes his hands first.

Grace starts the meeting by telling us that anything said in this room will stay in this room, and I wonder how she can guarantee that. Grace explains that at every meeting there is a draw for a ten-dollar gift card open to everyone who participates. I think about winning the gift card and I already have it spent in my head. I'd buy Nohkum one of her favourite books to read, one of those love novels with a picture of a muscular white guy on the front. Why she likes those, I honestly don't know. All I know is there are never any Native people on the covers of the books Nohkum reads.

Grace asks us to start the meeting by sharing our pronouns and one thing we're proud of. Ty says he'll go first.
"My pronouns are he and him and I am fucking proud I'm
still standing after everything I've been through." I kind of
like that answer. Maybe I can overlook his pimple-popping
and shake his hand. I don't know why I keep thinking about
shaking his hand. Do people even shake hands anymore?

Rhys goes next. "My pronouns are she and her. Let's see,
um, I'm actually proud that I'm passing grade 11 and it's been
a lot better than grade 10." *Rhys*, I like that name.

Misty speaks up. "My pronouns are they/them. I'm proud
of my ability to keep people out of my personal space." Misty
looks at me as they say this. I look down at the carpet and
notice it has threadbare patches, just like home. It has to be
about a hundred years old.

It's Jared's turn next and for some reason he turns his
chair back around so it's facing forward; maybe because he
has something serious to say? "I like to be referred to as he
and him." Jared continues after a pause: "The one thing I'm
proud of is my mom. I'm proud because she's gone three
months without drinking... so far, so good." I'm suddenly
interested in what he has to say.

Grace looks at me and nods. "My pronouns are she and
her and I am proud of..." I was too busy listening to what
everyone else was saying to think of a good answer to spew
out. I take a moment. "Um... I'm proud of my nohkum for
taking care of us for the past few years. She made sure we
had enough food and love and support." I feel tears start to
form in my eyes.

Rhys asks, "What does 'nohkum' mean?"

I wipe the tears on my sleeves. "'Nohkum' is grandmother in Cree." Rhys nods and leans back in her chair. "Cool," she says in a quiet voice.

Next, Grace asks us to share how our week's been going and one goal we have for next week. Misty volunteers to go first. "For once, my week's been pretty calm, which isn't always the case. Where I come from was sort of fucked up, so... calm? It's a good thing. One thing I am shooting for is to pass my learner's test, especially since it's paid for by the Ministry." I file that in my head as something to ask the Cheshire Cat about.

Jared goes next. "How's my week going? Well, I've definitely seen worse. Like Misty says, it feels good to have a calm week. It feels really good not to be worried about my mom and if she'll ever come home again... yeah, I know that shouldn't be my worry... but it is. She's my mom and I love her."

I shift in my seat with a sort of excitement. Someone else knows how I feel. It's a weird thought. Jared continues. "I went to my mom's three-month celebration and it was awesome to see her so happy. One goal for next week? I want to ask my science teacher if I can retake my test and just tell him about what's going on in my life. Yup, that's it."

Rhys begins speaking. "Well, my week went okay. Actually, I had court this week and spoke for myself about how I want to change my life and how I wouldn't be able to do that without a second chance. The judge gave me probation instead of sending me to a juvenile detention centre."

Grace claps, which starts everyone clapping. "It's really great you used your voice, Rhys, and you were honest. Don't forget the importance of honesty."

Ty clears his throat. "Um, my week? Well, I'm still wait-ing to feel better. I'm taking a new anti-depressant and I'm hoping it works, 'cause I don't like the way I feel." Ty sighs and folds and unfolds his hands. "I—I—I just want to feel better. I remember as a kid I always felt left out and won-dered why I couldn't just join in and be happy like the rest of the kids. I think I sort of fell through the cracks because I didn't cause any trouble. You know that saying, the squeaky wheel gets the grease? Well, that wasn't me ... I just flew under the radar. Now I'm waiting for the Ministry to find me a family to live with. No one yet, but they are contacting my band council to see if they can find someone. Sounds sad 'cause it is. Sorry, I don't want to bring you down. The one goal I have for next week? To have faith in the universe. I'm grateful to be here."

When it's my turn, I look up and sneak a peek at every-one looking at me and decide to stare at the carpet again before I start talking. "Well, let's see, I'm not at home ... my brother is in a different foster home, my nohkum is in the hospital and I'm worried about her, my social worker is really creepy. This is my second time in care, and the first time it was just me. Now I'm worried about my little brother too. Yeah, so I'm here because he decided to walk to the zoo while I was at school while Shirley, uh, my mom, was passed out on the couch ... so yeah. It's been a suckass week." I hear a few snorts, but I know it isn't because of my week—it's because I said "suckass." It feels good to talk about it even though no one says a word. I notice that my shoulders still hurt. It's like I breathed a huge sigh of relief and my shoul-ders stopped tensing and started aching. Now I know what

Nohkum is talking about, with all her aches and pains. But I'm not old and it makes me smile to think of how Nohkum would laugh at me if I told her that.

Grace thanks us for sharing and draws a name out of an old plant pot to see who won the gift card. It's not me. Jared wins, and I'm sad I can't buy Nohkum one of her cheesy books to pass the time in the smelly hospital, where she's surrounded by people too busy to even have a conversation with her.

I go upstairs and take a hot bath. I notice there are pretty smelling soaps, bath salts, and bath beads and take the liberty of using some. I feel the heat surround my body and notice my shoulders feel better. I wash my hair with some coconut concoction and use conditioner that I pump into my hand. I give my hair a good coating like I would coat Nohkum's bannock with butter and lie back, the bubbles tickling my nose. I feel a little guilty that I am enjoying this, but I know Nohkum would want me to enjoy myself whenever I could, so I inhale the scents and feel the warmth take over and relax my body, making me sleepy.

When I'm finished in the bath, I crawl into the top bunk, hoping I don't wake up Misty the Terrible, who is snoring softly. For once, I don't need anyone to ask me to pray. The tears stream down my face and I silently beg that Nohkum will miraculously get better quick. I beg that Marcus is sleeping, full, and happy, and I beg that Shirley will quit drinking. I don't know who I'm begging, but if Nohkum believes, then I have to believe.

16

Muffin Tops and Nosy Noras

WAKE UP TO the sound of someone knocking on the door, and for a second, I think I'm in my own bed. I open my eyes and the ceiling is right there, I can touch it, and I remember where I am. My heart hurts. Heartbroken. What am I supposed to do now? I feel so hopeless and helpless. I promised Marcus I would always take care of him, but now I can't protect him. When he was little and Shirley was out drinking and Nohkum wasn't around yet, he would tell me not to leave him, and I told him I would never. A fresh wave of tears starts brewing but I don't let them fall. Grace pokes her head in. "Breakfast is ready. Get dressed. I'm driving you to school."

I spent most of the weekend in bed. Grace was like a pesky fly—she kept coming in and asking me to help with this or that. I got the feeling it was because she didn't want me to waste away in bed feeling sorry for myself. I should have gone to see Nohkum but that would have made all of this more real. It would mean facing that Nohkum is in the hospital, and Marcus is in a foster home, and I'm in a group home... and I'm really worried about Toofie but what can I do? I tried calling the house but Shirley didn't pick up. So instead of thinking about all that, I just wanted to sleep. Jared and I did go for a walk yesterday—well, more like Grace told us to get our butts in gear and go buy some milk and butter. But Jared's nice. He has nice teeth. Who thinks about liking someone's teeth when their cat might be starving? Me, that's who.

I get dressed quickly, grab my backpack, and join the rest of the house in the kitchen. I'm reaching for the last muffin when Misty swoops in and grabs it. "You snooze, you lose!" they say with a cackle.

Grace comes in and asks if everyone has made their lunch. I'm the only one who hasn't. I shake my head. Grace gives me five dollars and says I can buy lunch today. Misty asks if they can too. Grace says they know the rules and that this is a one-off. She reminds Misty that they got lunch money on their first day here too. Misty stares at me for a few seconds, then shakes their head, grabs an apple, and takes a crispy bite. Didn't they already eat the last muffin? Rhys gives me a look of sympathy. Ty takes an apple, too, bites into it and waggles his eyebrows. "Welcome to the flip side," he says as he walks out, looking at me wide-eyed. I take an apple and head out the door. Misty calls shotgun and I get stuck in the back of the minivan. It smells like old fries and BO. A lot of kids must have travelled in here.

By the time we drop off the other kids, I'm late for school. I hate being late. Everyone stares at you like it says they should in the school handbook. Gawking like they have nothing better to do. And there I am on stage, walking in with clothes I would never choose to wear but have to. I can't very well go naked, Nohkum once said, and I cheekily asked her why. Nohkum lovingly pushed my head away and said, "Netch." I asked her what "netch" means, and she said it can mean a lot of things depending on how you say it.

Grace says she needs to come in to talk to the principal, Mrs. Thompson. When we get to her office, she comes out into the hallway and tells me I should go to class. As I'm walking toward social studies, Mandy comes out of the washroom. She looks at me with a smirk and whispers, "I heard you're in a group home. I knew you were bad news." I push past her, not even caring that she drops her book. I wonder how she found out so fast.

Mandy's right behind me as I walk into class. She shoves me from behind so I almost trip, but I don't do or say anything as all eyes focus on us. Mr. Harris is talking about our next assignment, which is to interview a family member to find out where they or their ancestors are originally from and how they got to Canada. He fails to mention Native people, who have always been here. Nohkum told me "Canada" is actually a word from the Cree language, "Kanata." I like that. It means something like "land of the clean." *Good old land of the clean,*

I think. *Beautiful Kanata, where children are still taken from their parents.* I'll never win the poetry contest if I say what I actually think. I feel like a cartoon donkey, always down in the dumps with a fake pin-on tail, but instead I've got a fake pin-on smile. I stop listening to Mr. Harris and start writing.

FAKE PIN-ON SMILE
That's me
The one all alone
In the corner
Eating air
Because her shoes broke
And no one knows
What bannock is
Not even Shirley
Drinking her beers and whey.
While I sit
In the corner
Dreaming of a sandwich
Trying to pin on my smile
With yesterday's happiness
gone.

The lunch bell rings, but not before Mrs. Thompson's big announcement over the PA: "Nevaeh Brown, come to the office please, Nevaeh Brown." Mandy says to no one and everyone, "Must have something to do with the group home she's in for fat losers like her." Not everyone turns to stare at me, but some people do. Some of them smirk and others have pity in their eyes. Why is Mandy in all my classes?

I'm the first one to bolt out of the room, walking quickly to the nearest exit. I keep walking and walking, off school grounds and through the streets. I decide to go see Nohkum. I can't face anyone else right now, especially after Mandy's stupid pronouncement. Shame washes over me again as I walk and walk.

I take the elevator up to Nohkum's floor. She is lying in bed staring at the ceiling, but she sees me out the corner of her eye. "Eva!" Her face lights up and she reaches for me. I notice how thin her arms look and how the skin sort of hangs around her elbows. I crawl into her arms and she smells my hair. Who smells other people's hair? Nohkum, that's who.

"Why aren't you in school?"

I tell her what Mandy has done. Nohkum holds me tighter and says, "My girl, it doesn't matter what she says or thinks, she's not living your life, you are. You have two choices: you can let what people say bother you or you can choose to let it go. Don't carry it around—it isn't yours to carry."

We talk some more about school. She must know about what's happened, but I don't want to tell her that they put me in a home with a bunch of sad and angry teens. I don't want to tell her how worried I am about Marcus. I don't want to tell her how I felt when they took him away. Instead, I tell her I haven't entered the poetry contest yet, that I don't know what to write about. "You know who you should talk to? Your mom. She's the other writer in the family. I'm just good with numbers... bingo numbers!" I know she's trying to be funny, but right now, it doesn't feel funny at all. I can't even think Shirley's name without feeling angry.

The nurse pops her head into the room and tells Nohkum she has to go downstairs for X-rays. I get up to leave, but when I lean over to hug Nohkum, she stops me.

"One more thing, Eva. Reach under my pillow." I slide my hand under Nohkum's pillow and I feel a book. I pull it out and see it's Shirley's journal. I stare at it. I pass her the small, purple book. "Eva, I want you to read it. I want you to understand. I know what's happened. I know." Nohkum looks frail and sad and I can only nod. "Your mom brought it to me to read. And I want you to read it too."

"Why would I read someone else's journal, Nohkum, especially hers? Do you think it'll change anything?" I'm so angry. I'm angrier than I've ever been.

"She doesn't want you to feel like she doesn't love you. I think this will help you understand." Nohkum looks even sadder, so I grab the book a little roughly, then kiss her cheek.

"Okay, Nohkum. Okay." I take a deep breath. "For you I'd walk across the ocean with water shoes if I could." I don't know why I'm making some lame joke when I'm so angry and Nohkum's so sad. I want Nohkum to laugh, but she just nods and looks like she's in pain.

The nurse comes in to take her for X-rays. I say goodbye as I leave the room, and Nohkum gives a little wave.

I head down to the cafeteria. Grace gave me five bucks for lunch, but she didn't say where I had to eat. I order fries and gravy and a small pop. I find an empty corner and people-watch for a while. I set the purple journal on the table, but I leave it closed. I'm not ready to open it yet.

17

Abandoned Kidcats (Not the Chocolate Kind)

IT'S AFTER FOUR when I leave the hospital. I think about Marcus and when he swallowed the quarter and how he didn't want anyone to steal it. To a four-year-old, what better place to hide it than your mouth? I think about how Shirley is there, but she isn't really there, and now I've got her journal in my backpack. I wonder what it would be like to be Mandy. I bet both her parents are involved in her life and they probably always have supper together at the same time and every night it's roast beef with mashed potatoes and gravy with some exotic vegetable I've never even heard of and they never have to go to the food bank. Then I feel sad, like I've betrayed Nohkum, because she's had to wait in the food bank line once a week for years and has never complained.

Even though I need to get back to the group home, it's my real home I find myself walking toward. Our street is pretty deserted. I sit in my spot outside the abandoned house, listening for sounds coming from our house. Grace was supposed to pick me up from school at three and I wasn't there. I wonder if I am in trouble. Do kids in group homes get in trouble?

Rain starts to fall in tiny drops. Toofie comes jaunting over and I pick her up and hold on to her for dear life. I kiss her wet nose and she lets me. She purrs and my heart aches. I wonder if Shirley has bought her any food, or maybe even gone to the food bank to get some.

The rain falls harder and night is falling fast. I put Toofie down and walk up to the living room window of our house. It's dark—what did I expect? Of course Shirley's gone out; now she has no kids to stop her from going to her favourite pub anytime she wants. Shirley entered a wet T-shirt contest once and still has a picture of it in her room. I studied that picture once, mostly just her face, and in it she looks happy. Was it cold water or warm water, I wondered, and then chastised myself because why does that even matter? Shirley is not home crying or even feeling sad for Marcus and me. She's probably in another wet T-shirt contest right now, looking happier than she ever does when she's with us.

I start walking back to the group home. There are hardly any leaves left on the trees, and they lie on the pavement unattended until the street sweeper comes along to clear the streets of debris. Is that what the Ministry does too? Are we kids just fallen leaves, waiting for social workers to sweep us up and send us where we need to go? I start to wonder how Marcus is doing but I block him out of my mind. If I don't think about him the pain stops. It's all I can do right now... and that's enough. It has to be enough because it's all I've got.

When I reach the group home all the lights are on, and I see Grace's face in the living room window. She bursts out the front door.

"Where have you been?"

I try to answer and all I can say is "I—I—I" before I start crying like a big old baby. Grace comes down the front steps, puts her arm around my shoulders and gives me a squeeze, then guides me into the house. Rhys is sitting on the couch watching some reality show about outdoor survival. She says, "I'm glad you're okay. Grace was pacing a hole in the floor." I laugh a little, but stop right away, because maybe to Grace it isn't funny at all.

"I called your social worker because I didn't know where you were. You had me worried, Nevaeh," Grace says as we walk into the kitchen. I sneak a peek at her and she really does look worried. I wonder why Shirley never looks worried like that. Shirley wouldn't bat an eye even if I didn't come home all night. "I saved you some dinner. After you eat, we're going to talk." I nod my head and wipe the last of my tears before Misty sees me crying.

Grace places a steaming plate in front of me. She made roast beef! At least I think it's roast beef—I've seen pictures, though I've never eaten it before. Sure, we had the pack-aged roast beef you put in sandwiches, but nothing like this. Beside the beef is a pile of mashed potatoes with gravy that has congealed a little, but I'm not complaining. There's also a pile of veggies that look like baby cabbages covered in some kind of orange sauce. Grace sees me roll them around on my plate and tells me they're brussels sprouts with cheese sauce. I've never had brussels sprouts before and I've never had any vegetable covered in cheese.

I dig in and try to remember to chew with my mouth closed. The brussels sprouts have a weird taste, almost metallic. I don't like them, but I eat them anyway. Maybe Grace sees me grimace or something because after I swallow the last one, she tells me that I don't have to eat anything I don't like. She also says I can cut them in half. Great, now she tells me—after I almost choked on the size of them and only half chewed them because I didn't want them in my mouth any longer than they had to be. The roast beef, though, is as good as I imagined.

Grace takes my plate to the sink, then sits back down. "Do you want to tell me where you were?" I look down at my hands and notice my fingers have hangnails and start picking at them. She waits for me to answer. I'm not sure if I should tell her I went to the hospital to see Nohkum, because maybe I won't be allowed to see her anymore, so I say, "I went to see my cat."

Grace nods and motions for me to continue. I take a deep breath and decide that if she tells me I can't see Nohkum, I'll find a way to see her anyway. "And I went to see my nohkum," I say. I look down at the old table and see that it's made of real wood. Nohkum likes anything that's made of real wood.

Grace takes a deep breath. "I've talked to the social worker, and she's going to get you a cellphone so we can reach you when we need to, and you can call to tell us where you are or where you're going." I look up and for the first time in the past few days, I feel a bit of happiness. A phone? Like the kind of phone everyone has but me? "I know your nohkum is very important to you, so I think we need to come up with a plan for you to see her a couple times a week. Does that sound okay?" I nod and inside I am happy. I can't help but smile a little.

Grace asks if there is anywhere else I need to go or anything else I need to do. I tell her I am worried about Toofie because I don't think she has anything to eat. I explain that Shirley has never gotten Toofie any food. Grace says she'll get some cat food and we'll go feed the cat soon. I feel like hugging her. I almost get out of my chair but I don't. I sit back and clear my throat. "Yes, that would work. That would be good." Why do I sound so lame? Grace asks what kind of food Toofie eats. I tell her any kind. Toofie isn't picky. Toofie, like us, is just glad to have something to eat.

18

Brain Farts and Bath Beads

TODAY IT WAS like my body was at school, but my brain was somewhere else. I don't think I said anything to anyone, just sat silently in class and walked around carrying the purple journal in my backpack like it weighed a thousand pounds. I was waiting for the day to pass so I could go home, but why? What home? Where am I in such a hurry to go?

When I get to the group home, I sit quietly in the lilac room, then quietly at the dinner table. After we finish eating, I ask Grace if I can use the bath stuff in the bathroom, then admit I already used some, and she tells me that's what it's there for. So I take another hot bath and use the bath beads that are filled with some kind of oil—I know because I squeezed one and just missed squirting it into my eye. They remind me of fish eyeballs for some reason. I use the salts that smell like lavender and the bubble bath that smells like strawberries. *I am going to smell like a field*, I think to myself, as I lie in the bath taking deep breaths. I'm going to try not to think about anything tonight.

When Nohkum told me about the monkeys in my brain jumping from thought to thought to thought, she said sometimes you have to take charge and take care of yourself. So that's what I'm doing. I'm putting those crazy monkeys back in their cages, one by one. Gone is the monkey that says I'm not good enough. Gone is the monkey that says I'm fat. Gone is the monkey that says Nohkum will never get better. Gone is the monkey that says Shirley will never quit drinking. I sink into the water, let my muscles relax, and breathe in the warm, strawberry-scented air.

A loud bang on the door startles me and I hear Misty yelling, "How long are you gonna be? Other people live here too, you know! You think you can pamper yourself like a queen? Get the hell out of there! God!" I sit up and hear Grace tell Misty to use the downstairs bathroom and Misty whine that it's all the way downstairs. Grace says in the amount of time they spent yelling, they could have gone downstairs and been done by now. Grace reminds Misty there's no yelling in the house. I hear footsteps stomping down the hall, then it's silent again.

When I'm done in the bath, I walk quietly toward the lilac room, but when I peer around the doorway, Misty's not there. I'm a little afraid of Misty, but I'm not sure why. They're not bigger than me. I outweigh them by about forty pounds and they're shorter. But they don't seem to like me and it makes me nervous.

I take Shirley's purple journal out of my backpack and I carry it up into bed. I open it to the first entry.

Had a good day. Don't even know what to write but my sponsor says I should keep a journal. I have never kept a journal before. My mom got it for me. Ramble ramble ramble. I met a nice person at my AA meeting today and he asked me to go get coffee. I told him no because my sponsor says I should work on myself first before I think about another relationship. Relationship—that's a weird word. Poor guy wasn't even interested in a relationship. I feel kind of bad now.

Peter... what was my relationship with Peter? Nevaeh used to ask me about him. What do I tell her? Do I tell her he used to beat me while we were drinking? Do I tell her her dad was horrible when he was drunk but not so bad when he was sober? He didn't even remember that he tried to choke me... do I tell her that? No, I don't think that's something you tell your child, even if she can be impossible sometimes. I know she is hurting too. She doesn't even call me Mom anymore. Not since my mom came.

I used to be scared that my mom would leave, but something in her has changed. I see it and I am starting to trust her again. I'm glad Eva has someone to talk to and someone to teach her how to make bannock. I can't make bannock to save my life. Maybe it's not too late? Ramble ramble ramble. I think that's it for today, dear journal (ha ha!).

PS I have a job interview at the coffee shop around the corner. (Does anyone even write PS anymore? Ramble!)

I close the journal. It's a lot to think about. My dad used to beat Shirley up? Why didn't she tell me that? She could have thrown it in my face when I yelled at her that I wished I was with my dad and not her... but for some reason, she didn't. Shirley never wanted to talk about my dad and I always felt like she was keeping him from me. But maybe... maybe she was trying to protect me? Now, if I keep reading this journal, I'll know more about him, and more about her, than ever. What if it changes how I see her? What if I'm not ready for that?

19

Nohkum Almost Goes to Hollywood

AFTER SCHOOL I walk to the hospital. I made sure to tell Grace that was my plan when she dropped me off at school this morning. I do not want a repeat of her worrying like last time.

I think Grace might have anxiety too. Here's a thought: we all have anxiety, but some of us more than others. I learned in science class that fear is actually an automatic response that keeps us alive. Hmmm. An automatic response to keep us alive? How can my anxiety keep me alive when it feels like my heart is going to stop because it's beating so hard and I can't hear anything but the inside of my own head? *Boom, bang, boom.* I think the monkeys have cymbals now.

When I get to Nohkum's room, she's lying there watching the doorway and she sees me immediately as I sweep in with all my monkeys. Her face lights up and she reaches both arms out to embrace me. We hug gently and she smells my hair.

When Nohkum asks me how I'm doing, I don't tell her I started reading the journal. I don't tell her about Misty and their yelling. Instead, I tell her about Jared and his nice teeth. I tell her about Grace and the wonderful things she cooks. Nohkum says she wants to come live with me in the group home. I stare at her oddly, and she just laughs and launches into a story. "Did I ever tell you about the time I almost went to Hollywood?"

I shake my head.

"Well, there was this young man who had the brightest smile, almost as bright as the moon. He bought a car, a nice blue one the colour of the sky on a clear day. He was what you young girls call... hot."

I shift a little, then look into her eyes and giggle. Her eyes smile back at me. "Well, one day soon after I get out of residential school he comes driving up the road. I don't have anything to do, so when he asks me to go to Hollywood, I say sure, pack a few things, and jump in the car."

Nohkum is silent so I gently ask, "Then what?"

Nohkum continues, "Well, here comes the almost part—we make it to Vancouver and we party for a few days, then end up selling the car and going to Seattle!" Nohkum is laughing so I laugh too. "I still have the Seattle T-shirt somewhere." Nohkum laughs hard and clutches her side with a sharp intake of hospital air. "Ow weeya! Ouch, I gotta stop laughing!"

I stop leaning on her and sit up. When I ask her if that's a true story, she says, "Are my eyes brown?" I nod. "Then it's a true story."

Nohkum asks if I have Shirley's journal with me and I nod. She tells me to take it out and open it to the last page and I do. It says:

God grant me the serenity to accept the things I cannot change, the courage to change the things I can, and the wisdom to know the difference.

Nohkum tells me this is a mantra they use in AA, Alcoholics Anonymous. Then she says people can use it even if they aren't in AA. She looks right into my eyes—and I know she means me.

20

Secrets Are Like Stars

ON FRIDAY, I get called down to Mrs. Thompson's office after English class. For some reason, I actually go. She tells me that a few teachers are worried about me. She tells me she knows a bit about what's going on. She tells me if I need any extra help I should just let her know and she'll help me. I just nod. I wonder if she knows why I'm in a group home, but I don't want to ask.

Shirley once said—and I will always remember this—that you have to treat people in positions of authority like mushrooms: you have to keep them in the dark and feed them shit. So that's what I do. I tell Mrs. Thompson I'm doing okay and I don't need any help at the moment. Then I leave her office and walk outside where the kids are swirling around like dry leaves in a breeze. It's cold, but it's not raining today. I find a tree to sit under and pull a tuna fish sandwich out of my backpack. It's got lots of mayo and salt and pepper, and bits of diced onion in it. Who knew onions in teeny tiny squares could make a tuna fish sandwich taste so good? Grace, that's who. I take out Shirley's journal, open it up, and get mayo on the page. I lick it off and begin to read.

I'm happy my mom's here now and that she takes care of us. But sometimes I want to tell Eva and Marcus that their nohkum was a bad parent. She wasn't even around when I was a kid. I want to tell Eva her precious nohkum isn't a saint like she thinks she is. But I don't. I don't want to break my kids' hearts any more than they already have been... by me.

I was in care for most of my life. I never really got to know my mom until I was an adult. And now she's here, but we still don't talk. Have never talked about anything important. Haven't talked about why I was in care. Haven't talked about my dad. It's like it never happened.

Sometimes I feel like such a failure and a bad mother and I find comfort in booze, but the next day it brings me lower than the day before. What a vicious cycle. How do I stop it? My sponsor says relapse is a part of recovery, but that just gives me a way out cuz I'm always relapsing. It's making Eva hate me.

I don't even know how to be a mom. It was easier when the kids were small—but now? How am I supposed to be a mom when my own mom wasn't there to show me how? I want to tell Eva I'm sorry, but sorry doesn't mean anything to her. How do I get Eva to stop hating me so much that when she sees me she leaves the room? I used to be her hero, but my mom is her hero now.

I stop reading and realize I've been holding my breath. Shirley almost never talks about what things were like when she was a kid. And Nohkum doesn't either. And I guess I haven't really asked. I knew Shirley was in care, but I thought it was like us, just for a short time. Why did I assume that Nohkum had always been in her life? Where was Nohkum? What was she doing? I can't imagine Nohkum keeping these secrets, but she has. I can't read any more now. I pull out a pen and my notebook.

> *Secrets are like stars*
> *Shiny and so far out of reach*
> *When they die out*
> *No one remembers*
> *Except the person who lied.*

THE REST OF THE DAY goes by so slowly. I feel like I'm trapped in my own brain and all I can think about is Nohkum and her secrets.

After dinner, we have our Friday night meeting. Everyone but Misty is there. I space out and only catch bits and pieces of what everyone is saying. I'm chewing on my nails, thinking about everything. Anxiety at its finest. Jared clears his throat and catches my attention: "Nevaeh, Earth to Nevaeh." I snap out of it. It's my turn to share how my week has gone or something I'm proud of. I'm tempted to tell everyone the story of how Nohkum almost went to Hollywood, but instead I just say my week has been fine. Grace asks me to use another word besides "fine."

"My week has been... weird, cold, wet, and sad," I say. Jared gives me a look and tosses me a mini chocolate bar, which drops to the floor. I pick it up to save it for later.

21

Everybody's Life Sucks

OPEN MY EYES and see the ceiling and groan before I remember it's Saturday. I don't have to face school, where everyone knows I'm in a group home. Outside of class, I didn't see Melody all week. Not that I want to see her—but I kind of do. Even though her mom called the social worker on me, Mel didn't. *Maybe she hates you*, one of the monkeys says, but I tell it to go back in its cage. I think I'll go see Nohkum today. I find myself a little happier at the thought. I just need one of her hugs.

Grace knocks on the door and asks if Misty slept in their bed last night, but I don't know. I watched a movie with Jared, Rhys, and Ty after the meeting, then slept like a baby. When I get to the kitchen there are pancakes and bacon on

the table. I see the food before I see Jared sitting there looking sad, picking at his plate. I sit down, grab a plate, pile it
high with food, and dig in. I notice there's real butter so I
slather it on. Big news: it doesn't taste any different than the
margarine we always eat at home. Rhys and Ty walk in and
fill their plates too.

Grace comes into the kitchen and asks if Rhys, Ty, or
Jared knows where Misty is or saw them last night. Jared
shakes his head and continues to make his plate a playground
for his bacon. Ty and Rhys both mumble a quiet "nope." I
get the feeling this isn't the first time Misty's disappeared
for the night.

Grace notices the look on Jared's face and asks him what's
wrong. He sighs. "My mom is drinking again. I called her last
night and she sounded out of it."

Grace sits down and reaches for his hand. "Relapse is a
part of recovery," she says.

There's that phrase again. I clear my throat. "What does
that mean, 'relapse is a part of recovery'?"

Grace starts to answer, but Jared pipes up. "It means that
my mom will fall into her old patterns and drink again. I
hope it's only a relapse, a temporary thing, and not her just
giving up."

Grace says, "Relapse is a slip with alcohol or drugs. It's
part of recovery to expect the slips. Sometimes when people try to stop drinking or using drugs, they relapse a lot but
then their relapses come farther and farther apart." Then she
adds, "That is, if they're ready to quit."

I'm not sure if Shirley is ready to quit drinking. She definitely "relapses" over and over. Until I started reading her

journal, I thought that all Shirley wanted to do was drink and that she could freely choose whether to do it or not. Relapse is a part of recovery. Hmmm.

"Addiction is a serious illness," Grace says. "Recovery is not easy. It can take a lifetime." She pats Jared on the shoulder and takes a deep breath. "I have to run out and pick up a few things, like cat food and mayo."

"Cat food? With mayo?" Jared can't help but laugh.

"Of course not... cat food's better with butter!" Grace calls over her shoulder as she leaves the room.

Rhys gets up. "Have a great day, guys. I'm out like a light." Ty follows her. I've noticed Ty and Rhys hang out a lot. I don't think they are anything but good friends, though.

Jared looks at me. "Do your parents drink?" he asks.

I nod. "Yeah, my mom does. My dad's not in the picture. My mom drinks all the time, though. Does your dad drink too?"

"No. But I don't really know my dad even though he's sort of 'in the picture.' He has a new life, new wife, new dog, new cat, new car, and a new kid named Mimosa or Samosa." I start to laugh and Jared continues. "Actually, my half-sister is named Ambrosia, which is a flower, a wine, or an exotic fruit salad." I laugh again.

I tell him about Toofie and how I'm worried about her and that Grace is buying the cat food for her. Jared says he'd like to go with me to feed Toofie. I say, "As long as you promise to remember my cat's name and not butcher it. Even though it's totally weird, and like, not even a real name."

Jared laughs. "All right! I'm used to dealing with weird names, obviously. Come find me when you're going to leave."

After Jared leaves the room, I don't know what to do. I think about everything that's happened over the past week— and I decide to phone Melody. Nohkum says, once a friend, always a friend. I am either going to prove her right or prove her wrong. I think enough time has passed since our fight that Mel may actually take my call. Since I haven't gotten my new cellphone, I dial the number slowly using Grace's old-person landline. It must mean something that I still have it memorized, right? Mel answers after the three longest rings of my life.

"Hi Mel. It's Eva." I can almost hear the silence.

"Oh, hey," she says, and her voice seems so far away, filled with something I can't figure out, so I ask her.

"Mel, why did you get so mad at me?" Get to the point, like Nohkum says.

She clears her throat, but doesn't answer right away. I wait.

"What? You really wanna know?"

I tell her I do even though I know it's going to be hard to hear.

"I didn't mean to get so mad but... you're always so down in the dumps. You're always talking bad about people, especially your mom. It just... it didn't feel good to listen to you spout off at the mouth all the time. Or to listen to you complain about everything and everyone and... it was bringing me down too. Even when my mom and dad were separating, you still made it all about yourself, you know?" She stops abruptly, like she's run out of breath.

I don't know how to respond, so I just say, "Thanks for letting me know." It comes out in a whisper. I can't stand to hear more, not right now.

I am sad—and then I am furious! Who does she think she is? As if all I did was complain to her. We had tons of fun together. Does she think she's better than me? She knows my mom's an alcoholic! She knows I have to take care of Marcus! She should know how hard it is for me. All these thoughts swirl in my head and the monkeys are bouncing all over the place. I'm stunned. I sit on the couch in silence, letting them jump around in my brain. Doesn't Mel know that Marcus is gone, I'm in a group home, and Nohkum is in the hospital?

I hate what she said. I hate how she can't be there for me when I need her most.

Then Mel's words gently nudge the monkeys in my brain and they stop jumping, just for a second. It's like someone pressed pause. I never told Mel everything that was going wrong in my life because I didn't want her to know. And I realize, no matter how hard things were for me, she needed me too.

I walk down the hall to the room with the computers and there's no one in there. I sit down and write Mel an email. I almost never email anyone, but sending a DM would be too quick and scary.

From: HeavenNevaeh@sparkmail.ca
To: theoneandonlymel@sparkmail.ca
Subject: I'm sorry

I'm so sorry, Mel. Can you forgive me?

XO Eva

I leave it in my drafts. Maybe I'll send it. Maybe I never will.

———

LATER IN THE AFTERNOON, Grace asks if I want to go feed Toofie. We make a plan: Grace will park down the street from my house and I'll feed Toofie at the abandoned house next door. I find Jared in his room and tell him it's time to go.

When Grace parks, Jared and I hop out of the van. As soon as we get to the abandoned house, I call for Toofie but she doesn't come. I call her again and I think about how Shirley doesn't like Toofie and maybe she hasn't even been letting her inside. My breath swirls in the cold air. Jared looks at me. I don't know if it's pity I see in his eyes, but I don't like it.

After almost twenty minutes, there's still no Toofie. I fill the tiny bowl I brought with us with kibble and set it under the steps. Tears start to bubble up in my eyes from somewhere inside me that hurts, maybe my heart. I picture a smooth red heart with a jagged line through the middle. But then I think about a picture of a real heart I saw in my science book and it looked nothing like those idiotic red and pink emoji hearts. What a scam.

Jared puts his hand on my shoulder and says we should go because Grace is waiting. I shrug off his hand and walk back to the van and I can't help it—I start bawling in front of Grace and Jared and I don't care anymore. I have no tissues so I wipe my tears and—yes, gross—snot on the sleeve of my hoodie and I remember Nohkum bought me this hoodie from a garage sale. It has a faded picture of an old band I don't even know but Nohkum loves. Grace and Jared are quiet on the ride back to the house.

When we pull up, Misty is sitting on the front steps. They look at my swollen red face and don't say a word. In my mind, I dare them to say something, but they don't. They don't even look happy about my misery.

22

A Phone With a Side of the Nineties

O N MONDAY MORNING, I have to stay home from school to meet with the Cheshire Cat. I know it's about my new cellphone and my visits with Marcus. Last night, Grace got me to write down a list of questions so I won't forget what I want to ask.

I told Grace about the monkeys in my brain, and she really listened. I told her how I imagine they have little beds and how they bounce on the beds like they're trampolines. I thought Grace would think I was crazy, but she just said it was the best explanation of negative thoughts she'd ever heard. She gave me a hug and said I could talk to her about anything.

I let out a big sigh. "I think I hate the social worker because she always has this smile on her face like the Cheshire Cat in *Alice in Wonderland*. I hate how she never stops smiling! It feels like she's mocking me, so... I call her the Cheshire Cat... not to her face or anything, but... "

"That is one scary smile!" Grace said, and she laughed just like Nohkum, with her mid-section bouncing. I feel so much lighter today.

When the Cheshire Cat arrives, we go into the living room. Before she sits down, she looks around and dusts off the seat of the chair. I want to tell her that's rude and germs can live through a couple of hand swipes, but I don't.

"Hi Eva, you look good. How have you been?" she asks, with that smile on her face. Why is she calling me Eva? Only people I care about can call me that.

"I'm okay," I say in her direction, without looking at her.

"Good, good." She looks away and makes small talk with Grace about my clothing allowance cheque, then turns back to me.

"Eva, your first visit with your mom and brother is scheduled for next Saturday at the visitation office." Suddenly, I am seething. No matter how much I want to see Marcus, I do not want to see Shirley. I don't say anything.

"Do you have any questions for me, about the visit or anything else?"

"When can we go home?" I ask, my voice shaky with emotion. I hold my breath.

"When things are safe for you and your brother to be there," she says. She says it nicely, but in a snappy tone I ask her what that means. Grace places her hand on mine for a second.

"Well, there are some things your mom has to do before we can even consider you going home," she says. Her smile has faded a bit, but she doesn't seem upset.

"Like what?"

"Well, you're aware of your mom's drinking problem. She needs to do some work around that. She's in contact with me every two days and she is trying, Eva, I promise you. She's going to meetings and... well, I'll stop there. You should hear these things from your mom."

"But if Nohkum was home, we could go back?"

"That wouldn't fix your mom's drinking problem, but we would consider it if there were safety measures in place. Let's just see how things go."

"Safety measures? What kind of safety measures? My nohkum is the safest person in the world!" I can feel myself getting angrier and angrier.

"Eva, we know your grandma has been the main caregiver in your lives, but at this point she's in the hospital trying to heal. It may take some time. Even when your grandma is there, it's not good when your mom drinks and causes trouble at home. I've talked to your grandma and she told me there have been times when they've argued in front of you when your mom was drinking." I can't believe Nohkum would tell the Cheshire Cat anything about us! I can't believe she would betray me like that!

My body is shaking and I have to remind myself to breathe. Grace places her hand on my shoulder.

The Cheshire Cat reaches into her bag and pulls out a box. I am so upset that I don't even care about getting a stupid phone. She opens the box and pulls out a flip phone. A bloody flip phone. No one uses flip phones anymore besides old grandmas—except mine, because we can't afford even that. I walk out as the Cheshire Cat is explaining about the phone. No one uses a flip phone.

I stare up at the ceiling from the top bunk. The monkeys in my brain hop from bed to bed, crashing into each other.

———

AFTER THE CHESHIRE CAT LEAVES, Grace drops me off at school late, stupid flip phone in my backpack. I see Mr. Perry zipping toward me on my way to my locker. He's always moving fast, like there aren't enough minutes in the day to get everything done, but he never looks unhappy about it.

He smiles and comes to a stop. "Good morning, Nevaeh! We missed you in English class."

I mumble something about being late, and he just nods and smiles.

"Hey, how's your entry for the poetry contest coming along? Don't forget that I'm ready to read it anytime."

"I... okay, Mr. Perry. Thanks," I say. I can't tell him that my brain is full of all the things that have gone wrong in the last two weeks, all the things I want to fix but don't know how. I can't tell him that these days I can only write about my not-so-inspiring life. I can't write a poem good enough to enter in the contest, let alone win it.

As I walk to social studies, I think about how Mr. Perry is a good teacher. He cares about his students, about me. He's still bugging me to start thinking about what I want to do when I grow up. He stopped asking me what I want to *be* when I grow up when I told him I wanted to be an elephant. Now he asks what I want to *do*. I promised I'd think about it. What if I told him I think I want to be a writer? But can I write anything that anyone would want to read?

The monkeys, the monkeys! They start to have a party in my brain, and they're a lot louder than Mr. Harris, who's back to talking about our social studies interview assignment. I pull out my notebook and write down what the monkeys are telling me (before I put them in their cages... again).

MONKEYS
You will never be good enough
Why are you even trying?
Why do you even keep hoping?
You are too fat
One doughnut short of a heart attack
Why even bother to say no to an extra helping
You're fighting an uphill battle
Just eat it, you know you want to
Why fight fate
You were meant to be a fat loser
You will never amount to anything
So why do you even have hope?
Nothing will ever be the same
So just give up
Give up
Give up

Monkeys, go back to your cages!

I have no idea what happens during the rest of social studies class, and Mr. Harris doesn't notice that I've totally tuned out. The rest of the day passes slowly, and I walk home from school slowly too. When I get home, it's my turn to help Grace cook dinner. She's a great cook and doesn't need my help, but it's one of the chores we all have to take turns doing.

Grace shows me the secret ingredient in her spaghetti sauce. Actually, I don't know if it counts as a secret ingredient if almost everyone in the entire world has it in their kitchen—it's sugar! Grace adds two tablespoons of brown sugar to her sauce. I'll have to let Nohkum in on that secret. It balances the salt and enhances the taste of the bland tomatoes. I heard once you've had Italian tomatoes in the old country, you can never un-taste them, especially since the tomatoes in Canada/Kanata are sort of illusions. Yup, illusions of real tomatoes that actually taste like fruit... until we meet, Italian tomatoes from the old country, sugar it is.

I'm starting to get used to this new world where there's plenty of good food, but what I really want is Nohkum's soup and bannock. I guess that's what I miss most about home... well, not just the soup and bannock, but the whole process of Nohkum gathering everything she needs, preparing it, and all of us eating it together. Even though the ingredients in the soup are never exactly the same, it's always just right. I think of how the greasy goodness of the hamburger floats to the top, like it's waiting for you to dip your bannock into it, and my mouth waters. Maybe I'll ask Grace if we can make soup and bannock next time I help with dinner.

After dinner, I head to my room. Misty's nowhere to be found. They missed dinner again. I should do my homework, but I take out the purple journal instead.

I remember when Eva was first born, how happy and scared I felt. I knew I would do everything I could to make sure she never went through what I did. I would make sure no one abused her like they did when I was in care. Eva has asked me about her dad, but I don't want to tell her he threw me down the stairs when I was pregnant. I almost lost her then, but still I stayed until one day Eva got in the way when he was coming for me and he knocked her over. I couldn't help her right away. She just sat there crying mommy, mommy, over and over. I decided then that he had to leave. Everything seemed fine when he wasn't drinking, but alcohol always made him mean. And even after all that, I went back to him because I was scared to be alone. I finally realized if I didn't get him out of my life... I can't even think about that. I haven't told Eva any of this, cuz kids don't need to hear about those kinds of things.

I close the book. I think about how Shirley tried to protect me, from my dad and from the truth about him, too. And I'm sad. I'm sad she went through all that. I'm sad for us both.

23

Magic Pills and Magic Teeth

THE NEXT DAY it's finally sunny, but it's still cold. Leaves swirl on the roads and sidewalks, and people scurry along the main street, off to appointments and shopping, or maybe just hurrying to get home and back into the warmth. It is a bitter cold, the kind of day that looks warm when you're inside looking out, but when you get outside the wind bites your cheeks.

After school, I walk to the hospital to see Nohkum with my trusty cellphone tucked deep in my pocket. Grace told me to text her when I am on my way home and she'll come pick me up. I have a cellphone and no one to call or text except Grace. Would I even want to be caught texting on this dinosaur phone? I can't even get pictures!

Nohkum lies sleeping in the hospital bed, looking so small, so unlike her usual strong self. I stand in the doorway to the room, watching her chest rise and fall, and I actually imagine that she's dead. Who does that? Eva from Hope with no hope, that's who. I quickly banish the thought from my head and rush to her bed and reach for her hand. It is warm, wrinkled, and soft. She wakes up and looks at me and her eyes tell me she's happy to see me. She squeezes my hand and I want to cry. But I don't. I don't want her to worry about me. I want her to get better so she can come home, so we can come home.

Nohkum says, "Can you pass me my teeth? They're in the drawer there." She points to the beige metal cabinet next to her. I open the drawer and her perfect white teeth lay on a napkin, instead of in their usual plastic cup. I feel sad. Nohkum doesn't even have a cup to put her teeth in. She used to let me put the effervescent tablets in the cup of water with her dentures, and I would watch the bubbles rise and study how they stuck to the teeth. ohkum needs her cup and her effervescent tablets.

Nohkum pats the bed next to her, and says, "Come here, my girl." I go to her. My safe place, but it doesn't feel so safe anymore. I realize my nohkum is mortal. She could die, will die, and it's only a matter of time. I feel the tears start to gather. I turn away and open my eyes wider, trying to dry them out. It doesn't work. The tears fall anyway, making pathways down my face, and Nohkum sees them.

"Don't cry. I'm okay." I nod and think, *But I'm not okay.* But I don't say that.

Nohkum asks for some water and I help her drink from a transparent straw. Some water drips down her chin, and she says, "That's good stuff, my girl!" I smile a little and give her some more.

"So, what did the social worker say?" she asks, staring directly into my eyes. I look down and pick up her warm hand again. I trace her veins with the tip of my finger like I'm painting them a bluish-purplish colour and I don't recall if I have ever seen it before. Anything to keep my mind off of answering her.

I ask what she means and she shakes her head. "If I could get out of this bed and kick your butt, I would, and I will when I get home!" Startled, I look at her. Her eyes are laughing and she's trying to keep a straight face. "Are you doing okay where you are?"

I nod, trying not to cry. I've been doing that a lot these days, trying not to cry. I pause. I still don't tell her that I'm living in a house with other sad, angry teens. I don't tell her that I have to share a room with Misty, who has a chip on their shoulder the size of a mountain.

I take a deep breath. "It's good, Nohkum. I take a lunch to eat at school every day."

"And you're going to see your mom and Marcus this weekend?" I shrug my shoulders in a non-committal way. Nohkum adjusts herself in bed and I can tell she's in pain. "Eva, I know you're still mad at her, but try to see this is hard for her too." I swing my leg over the side of the bed. "My girl, you need to forgive your mom. At least try and talk to her a little bit." I bite down on my lip and wonder if I've drawn blood or if I'm just tasting salt from the tuna sandwich I ate at lunch.

"Have you started reading her journal?" she asks. I nod, but I don't say anything. "And? It's like pulling teeth with you. Now spill the fart beans." I giggle. Nohkum calls any kind of beans "fart beans." She says she makes her own bubble baths after eating beans. "Spill it, Eva."

"I've started reading it, Nohkum, don't worry. I guess I'm still trying to figure things out." I look at Nohkum and think about how Shirley wrote that Nohkum wasn't around when she was a kid.

She squeezes my hand. "I haven't always been an angel, you know." It's like she can read my mind. I look up at her. I can't imagine my nohkum doing anything bad. "They did some really bad things to me in residential school and that affected your mom. I didn't know how to be a parent. Still don't, but I try. Will you keep reading it, please?"

I nod and resign myself to the fact that I have to read it all. I'm not sure what else I'll find in there. I tell Nohkum I feel bad about reading someone else's private diary and Nohkum tells me Shirley knows. She knows I'm reading her journal? Nohkum says she's been talking to Shirley every evening.

"It's time to stop the secrets, my girl. Your mom has been through a lot and wants to get better. She has depression too."

"What does that have to do with me?" I say, a little too loud and a little too fast. Nohkum sighs and I stop tracing her veins.

"Look at me," she demands. "Eva, your mom is my daughter. She hasn't had the easiest life and she's done better than I have. She's made sure she kept you at home for most of your life. I made so many mistakes with her. We're just starting to talk about everything." I think she's going to say something else, but she sighs and closes her eyes.

She's quiet for a minute before she opens her eyes and says, "Eva, I ... I used to drink a lot, too, like your mom. If I could change the past ... I would have never let the system tell me I was no good for my daughter."

Before I can say anything, a nurse with little dogs all over her scrubs comes in and asks Nohkum, "Have you had a bowel movement yet?" Nohkum shakes her head and the nurse hands her a little paper cup with two tiny pink pills in it. "This should make things right again."

Magic pills to make things right again? Nohkum swallows the medication without water. And ... poof, she's still in bed in the hospital in a little town with us in care and Shirley running around with the most freedom she's ever had. We're in trouble.

24

Mr. Complicated

GRACE WAKES ME up at eight o'clock on Saturday morning. I hear Misty snoring softly and get out of bed slowly, so I don't wake them up. Jared is already in the kitchen, eating toast and jam and reading a book. Rhys has gone to see her mom and Ty is at a friend's place. This house really does have revolving doors.

"What art thou reading?" I blurt out in my best British accent. Jared looks startled, then bursts out laughing and I laugh, too. He's probably wondering if I'll make fun of him and decides I won't.

"It's a poetry book by a Native author."

I pour a bowl of cereal—it's the healthy kind made with granola. It sure is no Fruti-os, but with lots of sugar it tastes okay. "I didn't know you liked poetry," I say, mouth full of healthy cereal and tons of sugar.

"I don't know if I do or not. My mom gave me this book so I'm checking it out."

"I write poetry but I don't own any poetry books," I mumble through my half-open mouth. I think of mentioning the contest, but I'm not sure what to say about it.

"Well, you can borrow this one if you want." Jared watches me trying to keep the food in my mouth. "Didn't anyone ever tell you not to chew with your mouth open?"

"No," I say, and he says, "Me neither." We both start laughing.

"So, your visit with your mom is today?"

"Yeah, and my little brother."

"The first time I saw my mom again after I came here, I was nervous. Why would anyone be nervous about seeing their mom, right?" I nod, then finish my cereal and put the bowl in the dishwasher. I think how much easier things would be for Nohkum if she had a dishwasher.

"I don't really wanna see her," I say.

Jared puts down his book. "Why?"

I shift in my seat and fold one leg under me. "It's complicated."

Jared looks directly into my eyes for a few seconds and I'm uncomfortable. I shift again and put my foot back on the floor.

"Complicated? You're talking to Mr. Complicated. It can't be as complicated as my life. Did your mother beat you?"

I shake my head.

"Did she verbally abuse you? Call you every name in the cuss book?"

I shake my head again.

"Well, then what? Did she try to sell you into a child labour ring?"

I shake my head in exasperation. I know he's waiting for an answer, so I tell him about Shirley's purple journal and how Nohkum gave it to me.

"Have you read it?" he asks.

I tell him I've read a few entries.

"Any sex in it?"

I shudder and furrow my face. "Ewww! No!"

"Well, then what's so bad about your mom?"

Grace comes in and asks if I'm ready to go, and I am saved from answering Jared's question.

On the way to the visitation office, I ask myself that question: What's so bad about Shirley? She's never hit me, not like Jared's mom hit him. Sure, she's yelled at me and I've yelled back. Jared was removed from his home years ago and now he's a CCO. He told me that stands for continuing custody order, which means he's in foster care permanently. Unlike me, I think. I hope. What they don't think of, the Ministry and the social workers, is that even if they take a kid away forever, somehow they'll always find a way home.

I think about how Shirley sounds in the journal entries. Like she loves us, me and Marcus. I think back to how she used to try to get me to look her in the eyes, just hoping I'd hear her—then, one day, she just gave up. She stopped looking at me and we settled into a new normal... but is it normal? My chest starts to feel heavy with realization.

We pull up to the visitation office and park.

"Ready?" Grace asks, staring at me from the driver's side. I shake my head and get out anyway. We walk into the office. The white walls are decorated with pictures from the seventies, faded cast-offs from social workers who moved into new houses and decided to get rid of their grandmas' pictures.

The Cheshire Cat is waiting in the lobby. She tells me Shirley and Marcus are in the visiting room and leads me there. I peer through the window.

I've been here once before. The smudges on the window remind me how many kids have watched their parents walk away from them. I remember watching Shirley walk away, my nose pressed up against the glass, howling and calling for her to come back. I didn't understand why this place had so much power that it could stop me from walking out with my mom. I think I was about five, maybe just a little older than Marcus. He wasn't born yet, so I had no one to worry about but me.

Marcus is sitting on Shirley's lap and they're talking, about what I don't know, but she better not be promising him something she isn't going to produce. The Cheshire Cat opens the door and motions for me to go ahead. I take a deep breath and walk in.

Marcus jumps off Shirley's lap and runs over to me, almost knocking me backwards. He looks so happy and it makes me sad. Maybe he's better off with the foster parents than he is with us. I mean, all our food comes from the food bank and theirs is probably fresh from the store. They probably even have a pantry stocked with food. Normal people have pantries. Poor people have broken-down cupboards in need of new paint, or better yet, replacement.

When I lift Marcus in my arms, he feels heavier. I kiss his little face. I haven't seen this face in a couple of weeks, while we waited for everyone to get their shit together. Shirley is watching us but when I glance at her, she quickly looks down at the floor. The Cheshire Cat asks me if I am going to say hi to my mom. I mumble a quick hello. Shirley says hi back and tells me I look good. Isn't that something people say to each other when they don't know what else to say? How did we get so far apart?

Marcus leads me to a basket of toys in the corner. They're probably the same ones that were here ten years ago. The Cheshire Cat sits on the couch with Shirley and I hear her ask how Nohkum is doing. I listen closely as Shirley says Nohkum might get out of the hospital in the next few weeks. My heart skips a beat—only a few more weeks! I can survive a few more weeks. I decide to focus on Marcus and give him all my attention before we have to separate again. I look at the clock and the hands are moving fast.

Marcus wants to work on a puzzle, but there's a mish-mash of pieces from different puzzles littering the bottom of the faded basket, mixed in with figurines of firefighters and superheroes. We continue digging in the toy box and Marcus whispers to me, "Eva, when am I coming home? I miss home. I miss Toofie. I miss you." His little face crumples and tears roll down his tiny perfect cheeks and I hold him close.

"It's not going to be much longer. You have to hang in there, okay?" I feel like I need to hear this just as much as he does. Marcus nods.

Shirley comes to sit beside Marcus and starts to brush his hair off his forehead. I want to push her hand away and yell at her to leave us alone, but I don't want to hurt Marcus and I want this visit to be good, so I don't say anything.

We finally find a puzzle in a box and Marcus decides we should all do it together. So we do. After a few minutes of puzzle-making in silence, Shirley whispers, "I'm sorry." It stops me cold. Her soft voice and the way she says it makes it hurt somewhere inside. I think of how she wrote in the journal that she doesn't want to break our hearts, mine or Marcus's, but I still don't say anything.

We keep looking for matches in the puzzle. It's starting to resemble the picture on the lid of three kittens playing. I think of Toofie.

"Have you seen Toofie?" I ask.

Shirley nods. "I let her in at night and feed her twice a day. I read that animals should only eat twice a day." I wonder where she read that, because I usually just keep Toofie's bowl filled.

Marcus sits up and says his back is sore and Shirley and I laugh because he stretches like Nohkum does when her back is sore.

We continue to hunt for matching pieces and Shirley asks Marcus about where he is staying. He says, "There's a dog named Maxi and kids named Ruby and Tremayne and we play together."

"Are they nice to you, baby?" Shirley asks.

Marcus nods. "Mike and Verna are nice. They help me with my laces and we play games together." I am so happy to hear that. "But there's one thing I don't really like..." Marcus pauses. "I don't like cleaning my room!" Shirley laughs. I look at him and suddenly I see him as a person who can actually do things like clean his room. Why didn't we ever get him to do things like that? I've always just done everything for him. Now I can see he's not a baby anymore.

We only have about twenty minutes left, according to the clock. We're down to the last few pieces, and Shirley and I sit back and let Marcus try to figure out where they go. When there's only one piece left, I see we are missing a piece. *We are missing a piece.*

Marcus places his last piece, but there's still an empty space in one of the kitten's faces. He sits up quickly and announces there's a piece missing. He starts to cry and I reach for him, but not before Shirley picks him up and starts rocking him back and forth, telling him she'll get him a new puzzle. She dries his tears and kisses his forehead. Marcus lies in her arms and I have to just let it be. Part of me hurts because I am usually the one to calm Marcus down, but part of me feels relieved because I don't have all that weight on my shoulders.

Marcus sits up and asks what kind of puzzle I want and I tell him whatever he wants is okay with me. He happily tells me he wants a puzzle with a picture of a dog that looks like Maxi. I hope Shirley gets him a puzzle, but just in case, I'll ask Grace if we can buy one. She's taking me shopping for clothes after the visit. I hope she'll buy a puzzle if I put one item back.

The Cheshire Cat pokes her head in and says we have five minutes left.

Marcus freezes at the sound of her voice and jumps from Shirley's lap to mine. "Do I have to go, Eva?"

I kiss his sweet face and hold him close. "We'll see each other next Saturday, okay? You don't have to worry. Can you tell Maxi I said hi?"

Marcus nods. "And how 'bout Tremayne and Ruby, can I say hi to them too?"

"Of course!" I answer.

Shirley gets off the floor and says, "Eva..."

I stop.

"Is there anything you need or anything I can do for... you?" I look in her eyes and see how afraid she is to ask me— but she did it. I think about how Shirley was in care when she was a kid too. Suddenly, I feel sad for her.

I clear my throat. "Can you please look after Toofie for me?" She says of course and I tell her if she waits, I'll go get the cat food Grace bought from the van. "Eva, Toofie has food. I bought her some," Shirley says, and in that moment, I am grateful that something I love isn't starving, cold, and sad.

The Cheshire Cat comes in and tells Shirley it's time to go. Shirley asks Marcus for a hug and he runs into her arms. I see tears start to form in her eyes, and I have to look away because it makes me sad. No, makes me mad. Makes me mad and sad.

Shirley leaves and Marcus jumps back into my lap. I smell his hair and tell him it smells like coconut. He smells my hair and says it smells like bannock dough. Bannock dough? As sad as I am, I can't help but laugh a little.

The Cheshire Cat comes back in and says Marcus's foster parents, Mike and Verna, are here. Marcus starts to cry and grabs on to me. "Eva, I don't want to go! I want to go with you!" I can't help it. I start to cry too.

The Cheshire Cat kneels on the floor next to us and gently rubs Marcus's back. "Marcus, I promise you'll see Eva and your mom again next Saturday, and I promise you'll be able to talk to them on the phone during the week."

Marcus hangs on to me. I tell him it's only for a little while and Nohkum is getting better fast and we'll be back home soon. Marcus says he's mad at Nohkum for falling and breaking her hip. He thinks this is all her fault. From his perspective, it may appear that way. But from mine, it doesn't.

I take a deep breath and tell Marcus we'll talk on the phone. I pull out my dinosaur cellphone to show him and he grabs it from me wide-eyed. He says he wants a cellphone too. His foster parents poke their heads into the room. When Marcus sees them, he runs to them, which hurts and feels good at the same time. Mike tousles Marcus's hair and says, "Let's go, champ," and off they go. I wait for a minute, then take a deep breath, stand up, and leave the room without looking at the Cheshire Cat. I can't face her smile right now.

25

Mall Monsters Are Real

O N THE DRIVE to the mall, Grace asks if I'm okay. I shake my head. She puts her hand on my shoulder and says, "Chin up, Nevaeh. Things will get better, I promise. Ever heard of shopping therapy?"

I look at Grace. The old-school language she uses reminds me of Nohkum. *Chin up?* Nohkum has said that to me before and it really doesn't make sense. As if those two words could ever stop you from feeling sad. And as if I've ever been on a shopping spree. I mean, unless you count the times I was allowed to spend five dollars at the dollar store, and we haven't even done that in a while. Five dollars doesn't go very far, even at the dollar store. And you have to remember the taxes, so technically you can get four things, not five, like you might think.

We arrive at the mall and the parking lot is full. The wipers have me mesmerized as a slow drizzle gently peppers the windshield. Grace asks if I'm ready and we get out of the van. Grace has her trusty umbrella, but I don't mind the rain. There's something peaceful about the tiny droplets of rain on my face. Not the torrential downpour kind of rain, but the kind that gently hits your skin with little stings of cold. It's one of my favourite things.

Inside, little kids, parents, grandparents, teenagers, and wannabe teenagers roam the mall in small packs. I am conscious of how I look walking beside Grace. Grace is white and I'm Native, half-Native anyway, but I look more like my mom.

First, we go to a children's store with sizes 0 to 16. I'm pretty sure we're not going to find anything that will fit me in a store that caters to rich kids. Their parents can afford fancy clothes to fit their lithe bodies and the fancy food that keeps them that way.

The saleswoman asks if we need help. Grace tells her we're shopping for clothes for me. The saleswoman looks me up and down with an uneasy look on her face and says, "I don't think you'll find anything in the store that will fit her large frame. There is a store that caters to big-boned women..."

Grace puts her hand up to stop her from going any further. "I don't believe I asked for your opinion on where we should go," Grace says in a tone that makes the saleswoman cross her arms and step back, looking at the floor as she stammers out an apology. Grace tells me we're leaving and going to another store where she hopes the salespeople know how to treat people better. I follow behind Grace, knowing the other customers are staring at us as we walk out. I feel a blanket of shame fall over my shoulders. This shopping therapy trip is off to a very bad start.

As we walk away, Grace apologizes and says we shouldn't even have gone in because that's a children's store, but the "50 Percent Off" sign caught her eye. I tell her it's okay and we move on to the next store, which has Top 40 blaring. The clothes, displayed on mannequins throughout the store, are really cool. When the salesperson asks if we need any help, Grace looks at me and tells her we're okay. Grace tells me to go look around the store, so I do.

I find a few cute tops and some T-shirts and a jacket that look like they might fit and continue to look around for pants. I don't know how much I can spend, so I decide I'll put back my least favourite things after I try everything on.

The rack of pants is bursting with bigger sizes, probably because no one my size comes in here, and I find some that I think will fit. How do I know my size when all I wear is spandex pants and sweats?

Out the corner of my eye I see a blonde head, and my mind automatically thinks of Mandy. I turn to look—and it's her. I'm trapped! She's with her mom. They have the same thin build, blonde hair, and blue eyes. Mandy sees me and smirks. I don't want to shop anymore. I have about fourteen things in my arms. I quickly walk over to the bench where Grace is reading a book and ask if we can go. Grace takes her reading glasses off and plops them on her head. "Not without trying those on," she says.

I stumble over my words as I explain that I didn't mean that I expect her to buy all this stuff for me. Grace smiles and leads the way to the dressing room. Could this shopping spree get any worse? I guess it can't be as bad as the time Shirley took me to buy new school clothes—two pairs of sweatpants, two T-shirts, and a six-pack of underwear—and her card was declined.

I try on all the clothes without coming out of the dressing room, hoping Mandy will be gone by the time I'm done. Surprisingly, everything fits. I tell Grace I'll pick two shirts and two pairs of pants that I like the best, but she grabs the whole pile from me, heads straight to the counter, and puts everything next to the cash register. Is she really going to buy all of it for me? Even the T-shirt that says, "This is my personal space, step off"? I smile at Grace as the salesperson rings up the clothes, plus some socks and underwear.

I don't realize it until we turn to leave, but Mandy and her mother are standing behind us. As I pass by her, Mandy whispers, "First time ever buying new clothes at a real store, loser?"

Grace hears her and quickly turns around. "How dare you! I don't know who you are or why you think you can say horrible things and get away with it, but that is unacceptable!" Mandy's mom asks Grace what the problem is and Grace says that her daughter is being mean and rude. Mandy's mom looks embarrassed. She apologizes and says she'll take care of it. She gives Mandy a look and tells her they'll talk about it in the car.

I take a deep breath. I wait for the monkeys to jump, but they're still. Being with Grace is good. She makes me feel safe. Not as safe as Nohkum, but safe enough.

26

Mr. Meatball

ON SUNDAY AFTERNOON, I'm getting ready to go see Nohkum when Jared pokes his head through my doorway. We aren't supposed to go into the other kids' bedrooms, so he stands at the door waggling his eyebrows. Who waggles their eyebrows anymore? Jared, that's who.

"So, Grace wants to know: tacos or spaghetti?" I'm folding my laundry and putting it neatly away, being mindful to steer clear of the drawers that are Misty's.

"Hmmm, ground beef or ground beef?" I pretend to think hard.

Jared says, "Going with the ground beef? We have a winner! Now what do you want with it? Tomatoes and parmesan cheese, or tomatoes and cheddar cheese?"

I throw a bundled-up pair of socks at him and it beans him on the forehead. He throws it back and hits me with a thud.

He runs down the hall yelling, "Spaghetti it is! Eeeeeeee! Spaghetti for Nevaeh!"

Grace drives me to the hospital in the never-ending rain. That's Hope in the winter; it snows sometimes, but it hasn't yet this year. I walk into Nohkum's room and gently sit on her bed, take her hand, and kiss her brown-berry cheek.

"Hi, my girl, so good to see you. You smell so good."

It seems like Nohkum is too tired to even talk today. I hold her hand and feel her grip loosen as she falls in and out of sleep. I sit and watch her for a while, then text Grace and ask if she has time to come back and pick me up. She texts back: *Sure, sweetie. Be there in half an hour.* While I'm waiting for Grace to get to the hospital, I pull the journal out of my backpack.

I can't do this anymore. Creator, help me, I'm barely hanging on. The kids are so excited about Christmas, but there's not much under the tree, only a few things from the charity place. Marcus asked for a bike and it makes me really sad that I can't be one of those moms that says sure and goes out and gets whatever their kids want. I can't afford it. Then Nevaeh yelled at me that if I quit drinking, I could buy him a bike. She yelled at me. Who's the mother?

My mom's bustling around cooking and I'm grateful they have her and I'm happy she's here, but what if she leaves? I'm not sure if I can keep them happy. I know I've messed up so far. Marcus would rather be with Eva and I know it's because I haven't been there for him. There's something inside me that always makes me want to run.

I feel it all the time like it's about to catch up to me. The only thing that stops that feeling is drinking. How does that make sense? I'm not good enough for them and that scares me.

The one thing I miss about Peter is he worked, and if he was here we would have been able to buy Christmas presents. I've tried to find a job and applied at lots of places, but with no work experience on my applications, nobody wants to hire me. Maybe I should finish my grade 12. Am I too old?

Shirley sounds like a regular person with regular feelings and hopes and dreams, so why haven't I been able to see her that way? Maybe it's because there's a lot I don't know about her. I think about it—she isn't too old to go back to school. That's something I want to tell her. I swallow the lump in my throat. It must be so scary to have kids. At least she's trying to figure things out.

When Grace texts me to say she has arrived, I kiss Nohkum's cheek. She doesn't even wake up.

By the time we get home, everyone has already eaten dinner. Grace warms up my plate of spaghetti and garlic bread and I tell her I am thankful she's in my life. She looks like she's going to cry. I stand up and hug her. She pats my back.

I tell her about Nohkum and how I wish she would get better because I want to go home. I eat my chewy garlic bread and the delicious spaghetti made with three kinds of peppers: red, green, and yellow, and that little bit of sugar. I can smell the garlic and taste the real tomatoes. When I'm done, Grace gets us each a slice of warm apple pie with ice cream that melts as soon as it's placed on top. Jared comes in and Grace serves him a slice of pie, too. We sit together, enjoying our dessert in silence.

27

Don't Focus on
the Bald Head

WHEN I LEAVE social studies on Monday, Mr. Perry is waiting for me outside the door.

"Nevaeh, can I speak to you?"

I put my hands in my pockets. I'm not really in the mood. "Do I have a choice?" I ask.

"You do, but I'd really like to speak with you," he says calmly. "You can leave anytime if you don't like what you're hearing. Okay?"

I nod and follow him. Of course, Mandy is in the hall. She stops to whisper to her sidekicks, something about me I'm sure, but this morning I don't even care. I think of how Nohkum told me to hold my head up high, and that's what I do.

When we get to Mr. Perry's classroom, he motions for me to sit down. He pulls his chair out from behind his desk and sits directly in front of me. This seems so weird because he usually sits behind his desk. He leans forward, his elbows resting on his knees. "Nevaeh, I know you've been going through a hard time." I nod. He sounds concerned and I'm not sure where this is going. "I know Mrs. Thompson offered to help if she can, and I want you to know that if you ever need help or have any questions, you can come to me too."

I stare at him. He is almost bald and I'm distracted by the little hairs that seem to wave every time he moves his head. *Focus, Eva*, I tell myself. Mr. Perry lets out a huge sigh. "I wanted to tell you that I was raised in care. I went to eighteen different foster homes." He stops and looks directly at me, but I stare down at the floor. He continues. "I know it isn't easy and I want you to know I get what you're going through. Maybe not everything, but a big part of it. I want you to know it gets easier when you get older, and one day, you'll look back at all this and it will only be a blip in your life. High school won't matter as much in the future as it seems to now."

I nod again. I twist my fingers together and rub the callous on the palm of my right hand over and over.

"So, I wanted to talk to you about getting your credits this year. I really want you to think about working hard now so you can move on and look forward to graduating in a few years. I've spoken to your other teachers and we've decided to make things a bit easier on you. Your grade in English class is almost failing right now, but I'm willing to pass you if you write a poem to enter in the *Medicine Wheel* poetry contest. The deadline is the end of next week."

I keep my eyes on the floor and notice how worn it is, just like at home, just like at Grace's. "And Mr. Harris will raise your grade in social studies if you do a good job with your interview assignment." He stops. "Please take this opportunity, Nevaeh."

I sigh and I look him in the eyes. He seems more than human now, an old soul like Nohkum. I sigh again and say okay, then get up and walk out the door. He calls after me that the poem needs to be handed in by next Thursday and the assignment the following Wednesday. He also yells out, "I believe in you!" It's kind of cheesy, but I don't know. It's something. And I believe him... I believe that he believes in me.

Of course, Mandy is standing near Mr. Perry's classroom, across from the office.

"Hey Nevaeh, something smells in here. I think it's you."

I look at her and her little clique. I stop and face them and say, "It's your upper lip, 'cause nothing but shit comes out of your mouth." I hear laughter in the hallway; even one of Mandy's friends laughs. Mandy shoots her an evil look.

She's about to say something clever, I'm sure, when Mrs. Thompson comes into the hall. "Mandy, could you join me in my office?" Mandy looks around uncomfortably and follows the principal. Her followers scatter and I walk away.

———

WHEN I GET HOME FROM SCHOOL, the house is quiet. I climb into bed with the journal and take a hidden chocolate bar out from under my pillow. Sometimes I need to bury my feelings under food. Good food, like chocolate bars. The sweet taste of chocolate. I read that eating can boost your mood. It's not my fault I want to feel better (or so I tell myself). I open the journal.

I don't know why Eva hates me so much. It makes me really sad. She used to love me so much that she couldn't be away from me. I left my job because she cried too much when I took her to daycare. I wasn't going to let my baby stay there if she was going to cry all day.

It was really hard after Peter and I broke up, but I couldn't let him be around Nevaeh if he was going to hurt me, or maybe hurt her. I always tried to get him to calm down because he scared her so much when he was yelling. She'd always reach for me but I couldn't go to her, because what if I had her in my arms and he decided to hit me? He'd get so angry when I told him he couldn't spend the last of the money on alcohol because I needed it for Eva. I was sad after he left but I had to protect Eva. At least when he was gone, she felt safe again.

I put down the journal so I can wipe my eyes. She wanted to protect me. It's in the journal, over and over again. Shirley wanted to protect me. I take a deep breath and keep reading.

Alcoholic. It's like nothing can make me feel better or forget, except drinking. My sponsor says it's a coping mechanism because I haven't learned to deal with things in a healthy way. She says after we come from trauma, when we stop drinking it's like we're babies again, unlearning and relearning. Sometimes I get it and sometimes I don't, especially when the only thing I want to do is drink, when I'm mad or sad and sometimes even when I'm happy. She had me doing some breathing exercises, but my anxiety still feels like it's eating me alive. Maybe it is. Some days I want to just run, run, run, fast, hard, and run some more, run like my life depends on it, imagining myself feeling so tired after running. I've thought of ways I could just run, like hop on a train or take a bus or hitchhike—but I can't.

I am trying so hard not to leave my children like my mom left me. She left me when I was six, and I didn't see her again 'til I was an adult. Twelve years. Where did she go? When she came back into my life for real, she was sober and helped me with the kids. I never asked her why she wasn't there for me when I was a kid. I never asked her where she went. Too scared that she might run again and I can't do that to Eva and Marcus. They need her.

There it is again. Nohkum wasn't there for Shirley when she was a kid. Nohkum said she was no angel. But what happened? I need to ask her. I can't put it off anymore.

28

Baby Powder, Friends, and Humble Pie

AT SCHOOL, I don't see Mrs. Thompson, and Mr. Perry doesn't say anything about our conversation yesterday. When I get home, Jared is there and I ask him if he wants to walk to the hospital with me.

We talk about how his mom has quit drinking again and how he accepts that she might start back up. He says he feels better than he has in a long time. After he leaves me at the front door to the hospital I watch him walk away, head down, looking at the ground. I wish he didn't look down like that. I'll have to tell him to keep his head up so he doesn't miss something wonderful. That's what Nohkum always says.

I wrap Nohkum in a soft embrace and her hair smells like baby powder. I ask her if she washed it and she tells me the nice nurse dry-shampooed it.

"Wow, it looks clean, Nohkum," I say.

"Because it is!" she says, smiling her toothless smile. I miss her so much. I don't want to forget all our moments together. But I'm also thinking about what it said in Shirley's journal—that Nohkum wasn't there when Shirley was growing up. I stare at her and she says, "Take a picture, it'll last longer." I laugh a little, but I don't really feel like it. I pull out my flip phone and tell Nohkum I can't even take pictures with this thing from the dinosaur age. When she laughs, I notice she doesn't look like she's in pain anymore.

She asks how the visit with my mom and Marcus went. I don't tell her that it wasn't enough and I don't tell her I hated it because Marcus cried and it took everything I had to calm him down and let him go. Instead I say, "Marcus is getting bigger and can do a puzzle by himself now. That's all he can talk about is all the puzzles in the world." When I think about it, I'm hurt that something so small could make him so happy, but I can't blame him. Like when he tried to walk to the zoo. I can't blame my brother. I blame Shirley for being such a dumbass. I said it. A dumbass.

Nohkum watches me. "And? What about your mom?"

I feel a wave of anger toward Shirley. "What about her? She's not my freaking responsibility! Never was! She's a—a—"

"Stop right there! Do *not* call her any names—she's still my daughter and your mother. She wants you and Marcus to be happy, she wants to quit drinking, she wants to fix her relationship with you, but she doesn't know how."

In that moment, all I can think is how Marcus and I can't be together and it's all her fault. "But Nohkum, she's—"

"Eva." Nohkum uses a voice I've never heard before. "She's seeing a counsellor right now, going to her AA meetings. Her sponsor went to residential school, like me, and she understands. She's even taking a parenting course so she can be a better mom to you and Marcus!"

I stop. I didn't know Shirley was taking a parenting course. I think of the journal, how she said she wanted to protect me, how she couldn't leave me and Marcus even though she wanted to run away.

"I need you to stop being so damn angry at her, my girl! If you want to be mad at someone, be angry at me." Nohkum looks at me. It's like she knows what I'm thinking. "I wasn't there for her."

I nod. I feel my anger start to disappear as if it's flowing out of me in a slow stream, like a balloon with a tiny pinprick hole. "I know," I whisper.

"She was taken from me at six years old. How could she know how to be a mom when I wasn't around to teach her? How could I teach her when my mom was gone too? I made so many mistakes with her. Don't you see, Eva, none of this is your mom's fault. But it will be our fault if we have this knowledge and we do nothing about it."

Tears roll down my face. Nohkum sighs and continues. "I can't ask for much more from her—but from you? I need you to stop being so angry and hateful toward her. She's my daughter. She's your mom."

"Nohkum, you said I could ask you anything and you'd always answer, right?"

Nohkum nods her head. "Go on and ask it."

"Well, why didn't you get Shirley back?"

Nohkum sighs. "I always wanted to. I did. But I told you I used to drink too much. I used to drink like your mom. And the social worker told me to walk away. She said your mom was better off with foster parents. She told me a child didn't need an alcoholic mother. She told me I would never get my daughter back."

I swallow a cry of fear and pain. "Can that really happen? Can they say that, Nohkum?"

Nohkum pats the bed beside her. "I learned years later that the social workers aren't supposed to say things like that. I'm not saying that I was ready to parent then—but it definitely wasn't okay for a social worker to tell me my daughter was better off without me. Sad thing is, I believed it. You wanna know why so many of our people drink or use drugs? Because they take our children away after they've destroyed us. Once you take the kids... there's nothing left."

I gently rest my head on Nohkum's shoulder. "Things were different back then, my girl. Not as good as they are now. It's getting harder to make children disappear, poof! Like your mom. I didn't see her until she was eighteen years old." Nohkum wipes a tear away. "Forgive her, Eva."

29

Stank Cheese and Sweetgrass

T'S TIME FOR our Friday night meeting and I'm not looking forward to it. This morning Misty took one of my new shirts out of the closet and said they were wearing it. They looked me right in the eyes when they said it, like they were challenging me. I didn't want them to take it, but what could I do? Nohkum says pick your battles. I just shrugged and told Misty not to wreck it. I think they were a little shocked that I didn't react. They stopped in their tracks like they expected me to say or do something more, but I didn't. Maybe they wanted me to yell and scream or... I don't know what. But I've been thinking that maybe Misty's toughness is just covering up all the stuff they don't want anyone else to see, so I'm letting them win in small ways. I can let them have that.

When I come into the rec room for the meeting, Grace is setting out a tray of meat, cheese, and crackers. The lights are low and a soft glow comes from the lamp in the corner. Grace smiles at me and asks if I like cheese, then proceeds to tell me about all the different kinds on the tray. I answer her honestly—if we had cheese, it was usually the processed kind that's always on sale. Grace says when I grow up, I can buy the cheese I want to eat. I ask her how she's so sure I'll be able to do that. I don't mean it as a serious question, but she stops what she's doing, wipes her hands on a leftover birthday napkin, and says, "Nevaeh, do you know what a self-fulfilling prophecy is?"

I shake my head and she tells me that whatever I believe about myself will come true. So if I believe I'm a failure, I'll fail, or if I believe I'm not smart enough for college, I won't go. I ask Grace if that's also true for alcoholics, and she thinks for a moment before she answers. "I think if you tell yourself you're an alcoholic and you have no power to change that, you haven't given yourself much room to grow, now have you?" I think about how Shirley says in her journal she can't quit drinking. Does she know about this self-fulfilling prophecy thing?

I grab a piece of white cheese with flecks of green and red. It really looks like it'll taste good, so I stuff the little square into my mouth, but as I do the stench of something along the lines of a fart assaults my nostrils. I chew the cheese and realize things are not always as they appear. I spit it into a napkin, and Grace laughs and says it's an acquired taste. I tell Grace that this is one cheese I won't be buying even if it's on sale. She laughs again.

Jared comes in next. He grabs a paper plate and starts piling it high with a bit of everything until it's overflowing. I move my chair over near the lamp where there's a little table I can put my plate on. With a British accent, Jared says, "This is quite the spread, dear Grace, do you have any fancy dips like caviar?" I laugh as Grace tells him that caviar doesn't actually taste that great—and it's not a dip. Jared makes a face at me and I make a face back. It feels good to laugh.

Since the last time I visited Nohkum, it's been hard to think about anything else. Nohkum's not exactly who I thought she was. Mom's not exactly who I thought she was either. I pause. *Mom*. It was there in my brain without me even thinking about it.

Misty, Rhys, and Ty come in and grab some food. Grace tells everyone to get comfortable and that we'll be smudging today. I know what smudging is. I've seen Nohkum burn medicines in an abalone shell and use it to pray. Only Nohkum doesn't like the word "pray." She says it's too Western, but it's the only word she knows to explain what she's doing since she doesn't speak much Cree. She says the word "pray" reminds her of residential school, so instead she sometimes says she talks to the universe, but even still, she's doing it in English and not her own language.

Grace opens a bag and brings out an abalone shell, some matches, and sweetgrass, cedar, and sage. Nohkum has them too. I wonder why we're smudging. Grace responds to my thoughts like she heard them: "We're smudging today to get rid of any negative energy and feelings we may be holding on to. My grandma taught me how to smudge." I think Grace sees the confused look on my face and continues.

"My grandma was Ojibwe from Ontario. I know I don't look Indigenous. I am only one-quarter, but my grandma used to say one drop of Indigenous blood carries blood memory. Since we all carry Indigenous blood, we're going to smudge." I look at the faces before me and the only one who looks Native is me. I never would have guessed Misty or Jared or Rhys or Ty were Native.

Grace breaks some sweetgrass off the braid using a circular motion and places it in the centre of the shell, which she's using as the smudge bowl. She opens the jar of cedar and the bag of what she calls horse sage and places a little bit of each in the middle of the bowl, too. She says, "These medicines are gifts from the Creator for our people to pray with. If you don't like the word 'pray,' you can also say we are letting our thoughts and troubles be known to the universe." It's kind of cool that Nohkum and Grace think the same thing when they don't even know each other. Nohkum also says if you fail to teach your kids to pray to Creator, then you have failed them. I've never heard Shirley pray, but maybe now I know why.

Grace tells us she'll be smudging first to show us how it's done. Misty pipes up, "I don't believe in any of this," and Grace calmly says, "You don't have to participate if you don't want to, Misty."

Grace begins by washing her hands in the smoke rising from the bowl, then cups the smoke and brings it to her head. She gently touches every part of her hair and says she's taking negative energy off her hair. Next, she cups the smoke and brings it to her eyes and tells us she's asking Creator to let her see beautiful things. She cups more smoke and brings it to her mouth and says she is asking to say only good, kind things. Then she smudges her ears and tells us that she wants to be able to listen more. She cups more burning medicine and sweeps it first over one arm, then the other, and brushes off the front of her body, bringing more smoke to her heart. By this time, she's no longer speaking but breathing deeply.

Grace asks if I can help her and motions me forward. She hands me a feather that I can only guess is an eagle feather. Nohkum has one too. Grace passes me the smudge bowl and asks me to gently sweep her back with the feather. She tells me to dip the feather into the smoke each time I do a sweep. I'm conscious of everyone's eyes on me, but in that moment I decide I don't care and gently smudge Grace's back. Finally, Grace cups more smoke and brushes the soles of her feet and says, "Creator, please watch where I travel and help me on my journey."

Grace is looking at me. "Since you're already here, Nevaeh, would you like me to smudge you?" I nod and Grace gently smudges me, asking the universe to guide my journey and make my path a little easier. She asks for the people in my life to be safe. I feel like I have something stuck in my throat until a sob escapes and tears gently run down my face.

"Tears are healing, Nevaeh. Whoever told us on this earth that we shouldn't cry? Tears wash away our pain, otherwise we keep it all inside." Grace washes the feather in smoke and gently sweeps it down my head and face and taps me on the head. I wipe my tears with both hands and I don't feel embarrassed like I normally would. Instead, I feel calmer. I'm conscious that the monkeys aren't bouncing off the walls of my brain. I can picture them in their cages, sleeping peacefully.

I sit down and revel in the feeling of peace. Grace smudges Jared next, then Rhys and Ty. Misty shakes their head no. Grace starts putting the medicines back in the bag. Misty tentatively says, "Wait! Okay, I'll go. I'll smudge." Grace turns around, smudge bowl in hand, and motions for Misty to come to her. Grace smudges Misty and talks to the universe on Misty's behalf, asking Creator to take care of them on their journey that has already been so hard. I see tears in Misty's eyes before they quickly jump up and bow. In that moment I see a crack in Misty's tough shell. Grace smiles and we all laugh.

Then Grace says, "There's no wrong way to pray," and that shuts down our laughter. That is a huge revelation— there is no wrong way to pray. Mom has prayers in her journal, I think. I realize it's her way.

After the meeting, I go up to my room. I want to hold on to the calm feeling I had after smudging. I want to be alone with my thoughts. I realize that I haven't written anything in days, haven't really wanted to, but now I open my notebook to a new page and the words are all right there.

SWEETGRASS
Smells of lit sweetgrass
Burnt to memory
At Nohkum's house
Braid burning as she circles
East to West, murmuring a mantra
Prayers we all pray for

As she gets older, I pray harder for her
And feel the pain of uncertainty:

Keep our loved ones safe
Let us have enough to eat
Forgive my mom, who may not know
Instead help her to see—

Have pity on us, Kisemanitou
It's a new world
They do not understand.

The smell of sweetgrass
A memory
and a necessity to have
a braid
of sweetgrass
in the kitchen next to Nohkum's radio

Nohkum's soft store-bought mocs
Scrape
Always scraped
the peeling linoleum floor
Instead of deerskin on earth
Her whole world broken
Kids different from a hundred years ago
Nohkum's breathing is shallow
From walking
From praying
From begging

For mercy
For all the lost children
That roamed the cities
Journeyed the jails
Wandered the reserves
Searching for themselves
In places Kisemanitou's
Law doesn't exist.

Sweetgrass Sweetgrass Sweetgrass
Home away from spiritual home
As it burns and smoke rises
To the clouds where the prayers
Gather like troops of buffalo
Our prayers can't be stopped.

Our prayers can't be stopped.

I put down my pen and close my notebook. My eyes are heavy and for once, I feel a good kind of tired. Nohkum always talks about a good kind of tired, the kind of tired that seeps into your bones after a busy day. Since Nohkum's been in our lives, she is always super busy. I hope she feels a good kind of tired.

I hear footsteps coming down the hall and turning into the room. I'm prepared to pretend that I'm sleeping, but then I hear Misty's voice. "Hey. Are you awake?"

I feel like I have to respond. "Um, kind of."

"I just ... uh, thanks for letting me borrow your shirt."

I think about how they didn't really borrow it—I mean, I

didn't really have a choice. But I've also been thinking that maybe Misty acts the way they do because they have no one. I think about how alone I would feel if I didn't have my family. Maybe that's why I'm letting Misty get away with more than anyone else in my entire life.

"Oh. Yeah, that's okay." I try to hide my surprise that they're talking to me without shouting or getting upset.

"Well, anyway—good night."

"Good night, Misty." I hear them rummaging around in their drawers before they leave the room again. I wonder where they're going at this time of night.

30

The Second Coming

SATURDAY MORNING ARRIVES, and the sun is shining for my second visit with Shirley and Marcus. Grace drops me off at the visitation office and I can see she has other stuff on her mind: Misty didn't return home to sleep in their bed last night. I wonder when they'll come back.

While I'm waiting in the lobby, I pull out the purple journal.

As much as I think Eva and Marcus would be better off without me, I still try. Why do I still try? Because I don't want them to ever feel abandoned like I did by my mom. One of my biggest fears is that the ministry takes my kids and never gives them back and they think I never wanted them, or maybe they weren't worth the fight. I always believed I was bad and that's why my mom didn't come back. I never want my kids to think they're bad. I think Eva would be just fine without me... she already hates me so much. But Marcus... I'm not so sure he'd ever be able to forgive me. No point in thinking about that though, right? I have to do everything in my power to keep my kids with me.

The Cheshire Cat walks toward me and smiles when I look up from the book. My first response is to smile back, but I think it comes out as more of a grimace, because her smile stops dead. She opens the door to the visiting room and I go inside.

Marcus sits on the floor with a bag full of kid stuff from Shirley: puzzles, crayons, a scrapbook. Shirley's sitting on the couch, looking tired. She catches my eye and smiles. I take a deep breath and sit next to her. She asks how I've been and I tell her I'm surviving. I brought a puzzle for Marcus too, but I don't want it to overshadow Mom's gift so I slip it to the side of the couch where he can't see it. I'll give it to him next week. There it is again—*Mom*. That's a word I haven't said out loud in a long, long time. I can think it now, but can I say it?

Marcus has torn open the box of crayons and now he won't have anywhere to store them, but I don't say anything. He's busy drawing. I see he has the gold and silver crayons. I always wanted that when I was little, a new pack of crayons with the metallic colours in it. I tell Shirley it's nice she bought him the pack with the gold and silver, but I'm not sure why I'm talking about the colour of the crayons like it matters. She tells me she got a job and I ask her where. She says she's working at a florist shop and she's going to learn how to do flower arrangements.

I don't want to cut her down like I usually do. Maybe it's the journal. I'm starting to understand her. I tell her I'm proud of her. She looks at me and does a double take. I scoot over closer to her. She starts to cry.

Marcus goes to Shirley and wipes her tears. "Don't cry, Mommy, it'll be okay. Verna said it will be okay and we'll go back home soon, okay Mommy?" I also start to cry and Marcus wipes my tears too. "Don't cry, Eva. Come see what I drew."

Mom and I get down on the floor. Marcus has drawn four stick figures and something that I think is supposed to be a cat. Mom asks him what the picture is about. He says it's a picture of when we come home. Nohkum is better and we go to the chicken place and have burgers. Mom and I laugh because who goes to a chicken place to have burgers? Marcus, that's who. Marcus tells us that next year he'll be a big boy and go to school and says we can't cry for him when he goes. He tells us he'll be all right. I see Mom tearing up again. I pause for a second, then reach for her hand. She gives my hand a squeeze and holds it tight.

Marcus takes out one of the puzzles Mom gave him and I help him open it. It's a Starscape Man puzzle. He turns all the pieces right side up and says Verna told him it's easier to do a puzzle if you can see all the faces. Mom smiles and tousles his hair and tells him he's right.

"Mom." She looks at me, surprised. I haven't called her "Mom" in years. I'm surprised at how easily it slipped off my tongue. "Do you know when we can come home?"

She clears her throat. "I've talked to the social worker and she says we'll start overnight visits at home soon. Because I'm doing so well."

"Overnight? How many nights?"

"Well, just one to start. And then we'll see." Mom looks at me and smiles. She brushes the hair off my face and tucks it behind my ear. "Eva—I never meant for any of this to happen." She looks down at the floor as she says it. I notice how short she is and feel a wave of love for her.

"I know," I say, and I feel like I do know. The anger that I always feel when she says things like that doesn't come. She looks at me, almost studying my face.

"You've been so mad at me, Eva. I thought you would never talk to me again."

"That was before."

"Before what?"

I look out the window and think about the journal. I feel uncomfortable even though Nohkum said Shirley knows I'm reading it. Is it really okay?

It's like she can see my thoughts. "I know you've been reading the journal, if that's what you were going to say."

"I feel... a little weird about it. I mean, it's a private thing."

"Yeah. But Nohkum said I should let you read it. She read it first. I asked her to."

"So, there's no R-rated stuff in there? I'm not getting to the juicy part?"

She stares at me, shakes her head, and laughs. "No, you won't find any of that in there—that's in another journal."

I can't help but laugh. "Gross, Mom!"

Marcus fits the last piece in the puzzle and exclaims, "There, it's finished!"

Mom and I both clap. "Good job!" Mom exclaims.

The Cheshire Cat sticks her head in and tells us we have ten minutes left. Marcus sits on Mom's lap and I put his stuff in the bag. He sits facing Mom, his head on her shoulder, and says he wants to stay with us. She tells him we'll have a sleepover soon and do an even bigger puzzle. I sit down next to her. She pulls me close and I hug her tight. It feels so good to hold her, to feel her against me, and it makes me sad. I've been so mad and I've missed out on a lot of hugs. Mom says next time she'll bring us some pretty flowers. I tell her pink roses. She nods.

31

Creator, It's Me, Eva

WHEN I GET to the hospital it's five o'clock, but the sky is already dark. I'm shivering and welcomed by the heat that envelops me when the door swishes open. Grace made so many apple pies this weekend, she let me bring one along after I told her it's Nohkum's favourite. The smell of cinnamon brought Nohkum to life in my mind. She puts a pinch of cinnamon in almost everything because she says it smells so good.

When I get to Nohkum's room, she's doing a crossword puzzle. She must be really bored because she once told me crosswords are for people with nothing to do. When she sees me, she lowers her "Crosswords for Beginners" book and smiles. It's infectious even though she doesn't have her teeth in.

"What's a four-letter word for 'plant-watering instrument'?" She tells me she tried *can*, *cup*, *glass*, and *pitcher*, and I tell her to try *hose*. She says it's a good thing I came in when I did or she would have been stuck on that word all night. I kiss her cheek and she puts in her teeth.

I want to ask her about what life was like when Mom was a little girl, before she was taken from Nohkum. I've been thinking about it a lot. I want to know, but I'm afraid to know.

Before I can say anything, Nohkum asks me for an update on the poetry contest. She asks what I wrote about and I say, "Your teeth!" She laughs. I don't want to tell her about the poem I wrote after the meeting on Friday. That's the one I'm going to enter in the contest. I don't know why I don't want to tell her, except that it's not easy to show someone something you wrote about them.

We do the crossword puzzle together for a while. Finally, she puts down the book and asks, "Eva, is there something you want to talk about?"

I know she knows me so well, but I didn't expect her to sense my anxiety around asking her about Mom's childhood. I hesitate. She says, "Spit it out! I don't have time to guess!" Then she smiles.

"I—I—I, ummm... was wondering about... how..." Nohkum pats the bed next to her and I sit down.

"There's nothing you can ask me or tell me that would ever change things, Eva. Look, you know all about my past now. Just ask." I stare down at the thin baby blue blanket that doesn't seem warm at all, which is probably why there are two on the bed.

"I wanted to know... what was it like when Mom was at home, before she was in care?"

Nohkum smiles. "Oh, is that all?"

I nod. Nohkum says she smells cinnamon. I almost forgot her surprise. I pull out the apple pie, which looks a little beaten up, along with two plastic forks. Nohkum smiles and I push the rolling hospital table over her lap. She takes the first bite and mumbles how good it is. She says it tastes homemade and I tell her I helped Grace bake it. Nohkum smacks her lips and digs in, as she tells me the food at the hospital tastes like cardboard soaked in chicken stock. I laugh. She puts her fork down and adjusts herself, and I can see she's moving a lot better than even a few days ago.

"My daughter was such a good girl. But, Eva, like I said, I didn't know how to be a parent. I still cry about it to this day. I wish I had known then what I know now… something like that, anyway. She was always scared, and I can't blame her." I rub Nohkum's knuckles and pinch the skin gently between my fingers to create a little skin tent that doesn't pop back into shape like mine does.

"Do you know what day it is?" I nod. Of course I know; even my dinosaur phone can tell me that.

"For you it's just a day on the calendar, but for me, today is the anniversary of the last time I ever saw my mom."

I'm taken aback and don't know what to say. She continues. "I was only four years old when they came to get me and some other kids off the rez. A bunch of police, a priest, and a nun came to the community and started rounding us up to take us to residential school. I remember my mom crying. I hung on to her so tight and told her in Cree I didn't want to go. She told me she'd be in big trouble if I didn't. She was so beautiful… I can still sometimes feel that last hug. She used to cook with cinnamon because it smelled so good, so even if we were eating deer, it would still smell like cinnamon."

I reach for Nohkum's hand. Her eyes have gotten red like she's about to cry, but she doesn't. She just sighs and continues. "I left my mom all alone and never saw her again." Now she does start to cry. I move closer and hug her gently. "That's how I felt for years and years, Eva, like it was my fault she died. I thought she died because I broke her heart." Nohkum wipes her tears.

"It wasn't until I was much older that I understood. I didn't leave my mom, and she didn't look at it that way either. I never saw her again, Eva, because she started drinking and couldn't stop. She ended up dying when I was about fourteen, but I didn't know about it until I tried to go back home after I was let out. I spent years wondering why she never came to see me. Years thinking she was happy that I wasn't there. It wasn't like that.

"I saw a counsellor who helped me see that losing your mom to child welfare when she was six wasn't my fault either. I moved to the city and did a lot of healing, started to learn about our culture, met people like me, and we'd cry together. Your mom aged out of care and found me, and by then I was sober. But she was mad. She said I was living the good life in the city while she was in care. I couldn't get her to understand until I gave her my journal to read. By the time she reached out to me again you were about ten and Marcus was just a baby.

"Eva, how could I be a mom, how can your mom know how to be a mom, when my mom wasn't there to teach me, and I wasn't there to teach your mom? How can you teach something to someone when you don't even know how to do it yourself? At residential school I learned some things, like how to sew and plant a garden and knit, but I didn't learn how to parent or how to have good relationships. A lot of bad stuff went on there. Some kids died and some just never went home. I guess I was lucky because I made it out, but then I had your mom and I didn't know what to do. That's why I'm so happy to hear you call her 'Mom,' Eva. She's doing her best with what she knows, which isn't much, but at least she's trying. I want you to forgive her like she forgave me. Can you do that?"

I nod and she pulls me into her warm embrace. I point to her hip and ask if it still hurts. She says her heart gives her more pain than any silly fall ever could. I ask her when she'll be coming home. She kisses the top of my head and says, "Very soon, my girl, very soon."

I WALK OUT OF THE HOSPITAL into the cold, dark night. There's something about the night air, when I can see my breath, that makes me feel real. When I was a little kid, I used to pretend I was smoking. I watch my breath swirling up into the sky, which reminds me of Nohkum. Nohkum says the smoke from smudging carries our prayers to Creator. I wonder if hot swirls of breath count?

Um, Creator, it's me, Eva... well, you may know me as Nevaeh. I want to go home. I want to be with my Nohkum. You probably know she's in the hospital. Of course you know, you're omniscient. That's what Nohkum would say. I think it's one of the bigger words she knows and I learned it from her. I wish Nohkum could be omniscient. *If you could help my Nohkum get better fast and come home, I would be very grateful.*

Tears form in the corners of my eyes. I don't brush them away, and I feel the sting of the night air cooling them as they slide down my cheeks. *I want my little brother home. You probably know him too. His name's Marcus and he didn't ask for any of this. I feel so sad. So hurt. I feel broken. I feel like my life has been ripped apart and nothing will fix it again. My mom's an alcoholic and I'm not sure if I trust her to fix it. I'm not even certain she knows how, but could you help her with that? If you could help her to help us, I'd really appreciate it.*

It's so cold and I am glad for the jacket Grace bought me, but these leggings really don't keep my legs warm. *Please take care of Marcus, Creator, he's so little and doesn't understand any of this and I feel so powerless to help him. Help him to feel happy, Creator. I miss hugging him and I miss when he would crawl into bed with me and we would keep each other warm.*

A loud sob comes out, which I wasn't expecting. I look around and the streets are deserted so I just cry. Nohkum says crying and tears are good, and I remember Grace said the same thing when we were smudging. It does feel good to let out what I didn't even know I was thinking. Nohkum says pain and suffering is like a leaky faucet: if you don't attend to it and fix it, one day it will break and shoot water all over the place. I think this is my leaky faucet breaking. *Creator, I've been so mad for such a long time and I don't want to be mad anymore. I want to understand my mom, and if you could help me with that, for both our sakes, I would really be thankful.*

I am almost at the group home, just one more street to cross. *Thank you for listening, Creator, and if you could help me with these things, I would deeply appreciate it and do my best.*

As I'm walking up the front steps, Grace opens the door. "Why didn't you call? I would have picked you up." I tell her I needed some time to think. She nods and says there's supper in the microwave for me, and I'm grateful. I'm in a warm house, and Grace saved me some dinner and even looked worried when I came home.

I ask her if she ever drank before and she looks surprised. "Yes," she says, "lots. I had a problem with it years ago." I ask her how she stopped. She says, "I stopped running."

32

Hanging in There

I WOKE UP THIS morning and everything seemed to sink in. I lay in bed staring at the ceiling and with an outstretched finger tried to count those bumpy white things. It was impossible and I only ended up with dust in my eye. Misty hasn't been back since the night we smudged. I keep thinking about how there's more to Misty than they show. All that anger must be hiding something else.

I can hear rain pelting the window and Grace moving around in the kitchen. I think about what Mr. Perry said about working hard now so I can graduate high school, how he said he believes in me. I do want to graduate. I want to free my mind and think for myself, like Nohkum says. I pull out my notebook and let my thoughts fall onto the page.

I can only be me
When my life is
Chipped away   like old rock and stream
Will I disintegrate?
Will I be able to put   myself back together
Again?

Second chances?
I wasn't even given
A first.
How much do I care?
Do I have to care?
Was I taught to care?

Chipped away   like old rock and stream
Taken to another place
Perhaps to dream

I hear Grace call my name from down the hall. She knocks on the door and I tell her to come in as I climb down the ladder. "Good morning, Nevaeh. No sign of Misty this morning?" I shake my head and stretch and realize I am happy. Happy? Not happy that Misty's still missing, but happy I'm going to see my mom and Marcus and that Nohkum is getting better.

"Grace?"

Grace opens one of Misty's drawers, like she thinks she'll find a clue in there as to where they've gone. "Yes, hon?"

"Where do you think Misty is?"

Grace sighs and sits on the little chair in the corner. I hear it squeal from the weight of her frame, but I think she looks beautiful. Some people are not meant to be teeny tiny.

"Honestly, Nevaeh, I don't know. Wherever they are, I hope they're okay. Sometimes the ghosts from our past make us want to run and we don't even know where we're running to. I think Misty's like that... just running."

"You think they'll be okay?" I find myself hoping they will be.

"The only thing I can say is just pray for them. The ones who have been hurt the most seem to be the fastest runners... not to say you haven't been hurt, Nevaeh, but that Nohkum of yours and your little brother have given you so much love. Love keeps people hanging on, you know?"

I wonder if Misty has a family that loves them. Then I think of my mom. Has she felt like giving up? I know she wanted to run, but did she ever feel like giving up? The thought scares me. I wouldn't want my mom to ever feel like giving up, like she couldn't go on. It makes me sad. I feel my eyes fill up and pretend to yawn.

"Grace? Do you think we can make soup and bannock for dinner?"

Grace folds her hands in her lap and I notice how old they look. I see her in a new way, as a mother figure to so many kids, and I imagine she feels sad when they leave, especially if they don't come back.

Grace gets up and goes back to the drawer. I see my new shirt that Misty "borrowed" sitting on top, but I don't say anything. If Misty comes back for their stuff, I want them to have it. Grace is right... I do have Nohkum and Marcus— and my mom. And her. I have Grace.

"Do you think you could help me make it, Nevaeh? I've made bannock a few times but it turns out like hockey pucks!"

"You could make throwing bannocks! You know, like throwing stars? I think they'd make pretty good weapons!"

Grace laughs and I join her. Her belly shakes like Nohkum's when she laughs.

I stop for a second. "Hey, Grace? Do you think you could call me Eva?"

Grace looks at me with a smile. "Of course. Of course, Eva. So... how do you feel about the meeting coming up?" she asks. There's a meeting tomorrow. It's a big one, with the Cheshire Cat and Mom and everyone else who has some say in when or if Marcus and I get to go home.

"Um, I think it'll be okay," I say, avoiding her eyes.

"Okay? Just okay?"

I turn to her and see how worried she looks. I'm noticing faces and expressions now instead of always avoiding eye contact.

"I—I'm a little scared. I'm afraid we won't get to go back to Nohkum and my mom."

Grace puts her hand on my shoulder. "That's one of those monkeys you were telling me about, Eva. I don't think there's any reason to keep you and your brother in care. Your mom is doing everything she needs to do."

I start to make patterns in the carpet: you brush it one way, it looks rough, and brush it the other way, it looks smooth. "That's the thing that scares me—she has to do things right or we won't go home. It's like our lives are in her hands—and if she messes up... It's just—it's sad."

Grace pulls me in for a hug and I melt easily into her arms. "Eva, things are different now. There's more of a focus on Indigenous children being returned to their families. Yes, it is sad that they have to put conditions on your mom, but from what I can see? If it's worth anything, I think your mom is a survivor and so is your nohkum—and so are you. This time, you know, your family will break those chains of foster care." I let my tears fall and I let Grace hold me. Her embrace is soft and welcoming like Nohkum's. I know this is what trust feels like.

33

Waiting, Ready to Go

GRACE DRIVES ME to the visitation office. I bring soup and bannock with me that we made together. They turned out good; not as good as Nohkum's, but I brought some to give to Mom anyway. I think I'm kind of proud of myself, but I'm not used to that—feeling proud of myself. I have the poem that I wrote for the contest with me too, ready to give to Mr. Perry when I get to school. I'm proud of it too, that I could write about my life, and my mom, and Nohkum.

Grace tells me to call her when I'm done so she can pick me up, and says, "Eva, you know even when you go home, you can always call me if things get tough—not that I think things will get tough. I only want the best for you and your brother. Remember my phone is always on, okay?" I nod, unbuckle my seatbelt, and grab the soup and bannock. I open the door before the van even comes to a full stop so I can jump out before I start to cry. Why do I want to cry when people are kind to me?

Today it's sunny and there is a soft wind that sounds like someone whistling. I used to be scared of the whistling wind before Nohkum came to live with us. Nohkum sure has changed my life... all our lives. When I'm reading Mom's journal about how Nohkum used to be, it's hard to believe she's the same person. Nohkum says sometimes it takes someone a lifetime to change, but when they finally get it, they live their days breathing easy. Nohkum says she didn't know how to breathe before; she was always waiting for something bad to happen. I get that. My anxiety makes me feel like that. I'm always waiting for the monkeys in my brain to jump all over the place. But lately, if I pay attention when they start bouncing, I can get them back into their cages before things get out of control.

Mom and Nohkum are standing outside the building beside the mint-green railing. Mom is smoking and Nohkum is hanging onto a walker.

Nohkum's face shines and I know she loves me. Mom looks happy too, but a little afraid, so I do the thing I normally wouldn't. I run to hug her first. Nohkum tells me with her eyes that I did the right thing. Nohkum isn't hurt. She's happy.

Mom kisses my forehead and tears come to my eyes. I tell her I'm glad to see her. I move on to Nohkum, who doesn't seem as strong as before. As I hold her, her body seems more brittle, and I feel like I have to hug her gently. Nohkum's the one who hugs me tight and kisses both my cheeks. I smell raisins. Not sure why, but she smells like raisins. She has a Gold's Gym shirt on. I've missed her silly T-shirts so much.

I know for a fact that Nohkum has never walked into a fitness centre in her life, but somehow it's just the perfect thing for her to be wearing.

"Are you ready, my girl?"

I look at Mom and I think about Jared. Jared, whose mother hit him and who he still loves with all his heart. I have learned so much from him. I borrowed his poetry book because I want a reason to stay connected to him. After all, he's helped me see my mom in a new light. I feel like I've been an angry, selfish brat to her. Not that she hasn't made any mistakes, but I've made mistakes too. And there's someone else I need to tell that to: Mel. Maybe I'm ready to send that email. One person at a time.

Mom, Nohkum, and I walk inside together. I wonder why there's such a huge table in the middle of such a small room. There are already four people at the table: the Cheshire Cat (who isn't smiling for once), a woman with a laptop, and two others sitting quietly.

The three of us sit on one side, me between Mom and Nohkum. The lady with the laptop introduces herself as the meeting facilitator and explains that she'll be taking notes. She says she's a neutral party who hosts the meeting and moves it where it needs to go, so she asks for permission to interrupt to get us back on track. She says the meeting isn't about blaming or shaming—it's to talk about next steps. I like that. She asks us to introduce ourselves and talk about our best hopes.

The Cheshire Cat introduces herself as Irene Chester, the guardianship worker. She says her best hope is to return us to our mom. I wonder if that's true, and I wonder if I should stop calling her the Cheshire Cat and start calling her Irene.

The lady next to her introduces herself as Marie, Mom's family service worker. She says she's hoping to assist the Cheshire Cat/Irene in making a plan to return Nevaeh and Marcus. *I'm right here*, I think, but I guess she says it like that because we've never met before.

The other woman introduces herself as Mom's sponsor, Mechelle with three e's. In my head I try to spell her name with three e's. She says she hopes Marcus and I are reunited with our mom sooner rather than later, and she also says Mom is working really hard. I remember Nohkum told me Mechelle is an Elder who went to residential school, so she understands everything they've gone through. I'm glad for that. I'm glad Mom can be open and honest with someone who won't judge her.

There's a jug of water and a stack of plastic cups in the middle of the table, and suddenly I'm very thirsty. Nohkum is introducing herself and it's my turn next. I abruptly get up and grab the jug, but with more force than I mean to. I knock it over and the rush of water heads straight toward Irene, and before she can move out of the way, her files and pencil skirt are soaked. As I apologize, Mom runs out of the room faster than lightning and comes back with handfuls of paper towel. She offers them to Irene. As I apologize one more time, Mom puts her hand on my shoulder. "It's okay, my girl, you didn't mean to do it. You're nervous, I know. Have a seat," she says softly. I look into her eyes and I trust her. I finally trust her. She has my back.

After Irene hears Mom's soft voice, she looks embarrassed and says not to worry, her skirt needed washing anyway. No one laughs but there are a few awkward smiles.

After the water is soaked up by Irene's skirt, Nohkum continues. "I am here today to help my daughter get her kids back. That is my hope. These kids need to get out of the system, to come home to be with their family and not in stranger care." Nohkum stands when she says this, hanging on to the table for support.

Of course, I'm next, and I'm so nervous, the monkeys in my brain are starting to wreak havoc. Nohkum reaches over and grabs my hand under the table and I get the courage to speak. "My name is Nevaeh and I'm almost fifteen years old. This is my mom and this is my nohkum... grandma." I can feel my face grow hot and I look down at the table. Nohkum squeezes my hand harder and I look at her. She looks older than I have ever seen her look and I know it is time that we start taking care of her. "And my best hope is to go home. Right away. I want to be with my family and help my mom and my nohkum. We need each other." I see Mom quickly wipe a tear away.

Then it's Mom's turn. "I'm here today because I want my children home. I want to stop this cycle of our children in care." She looks at Nohkum and Nohkum nods, urging Mom forward. "I know I've made mistakes, but I've learned and I'll continue to learn. My children need me. My mom needs me and we need her too. My best hope is that I get my children home as soon as possible."

The meeting facilitator says next we'll each speak about things that are going well. The Cheshire Cat goes first. "I'm amazed by all the hard work everyone has been doing. I'm so impressed by the closeness of this family. I'd like to support Shirley in reuniting with her children within the next couple of weeks. Marcus is in daycare and thriving and Nevaeh is doing well in her placement. We'll have an overnight visit this Friday, as I've already discussed with Shirley."

Marie is next. "I am proud of how far Shirley has come and how open she's been. She's made my job easier. She's attended all her visits, meets with her counsellor once a week, and she's staying sober. She has a part-time job and is volunteering at the homeless shelter. She's even working on getting into college." I look at my mom, whose face has turned red. It's almost like she's never heard anyone say something nice about her.

Next, it's Mechelle's turn to speak. "I am so grateful I got to meet and work with Shirley. She's well on her way to healing herself and breaking the cycle that has plagued our people for decades. Anything this young lady puts her mind to, she does." It's hard to think of my mom as a young lady, but compared to Mechelle, I can see that she is.

Nohkum clears her throat. "What's going well is how hard my daughter and granddaughter are working... to heal themselves. To heal their relationship too."

That was quick and my mouth is dry. "Ummm... what's going well is that my nohkum is healing, my mom is doing way better, and... that's all I got." I pick up my cup to take a drink of water and hope I don't spill it again.

Finally, Mom stands up. "I'm finally seeing a new life for us and... I'm hopeful. I'm proud of my daughter. I'm proud of how smart she is. What else is going well? My mother will be home soon and I'm going to make sure she is taken care of. I'm also thankful that I met Mechelle. She's helped me so that I can actually envision the future." Never have I been prouder of my mom than I am now. Tears stream down my face and she takes me in her arms. I let her.

The facilitator thanks everyone for their input and all the positive things that were said. "Now, we will move on to concerns, starting with Irene."

As the Cheshire Cat clears her throat, I stare at the floor, heart thumping, monkeys waking up, knowing she could say something that will stop me from going home. She could take it all away.

"At present, I do not have any concerns," she says, and I breathe a huge sigh of relief. The monkeys settle back onto their beds.

We each have our turn, and no one has any concerns until we get to my mom. "The only concern I have is that my children have been away too long. I want them to come home." I let out another big sigh. I can breathe.

The facilitator says it's time to discuss next steps.

Irene says, "I would like to return the children today, but systems are slow. I think it's more realistic to aim for the week after next."

I'm shaking, but my heart is light. I am going home!

Mom says she will be cleaning like a banshee.

Nohkum says she will be healing.

And me? I'll just be waiting, ready to go when the time comes.

34

Sleepover at My Own House!

WHEN FRIDAY NIGHT finally arrives, Grace drops me off at home with my backpack filled with a few clothes, a stuffy for Marcus, and the purple journal. I get out of the van and look back at her before I shut the door. "Grace, thank you for everything." She smiles and tells me she'll pick me up just before supper tomorrow. She hands me twenty dollars and tells me to order pizza for my family. I thank her and again I feel my eyes start to water.

I close the van door quickly and walk up the front steps. It's strange to be having a sleepover at my own house. I'm excited, I think, but I know it's going to be weird to be home, especially without Nohkum. Everything was okay when Nohkum was here, but then she wasn't here, and everything wasn't... well, it wasn't okay. The monkeys are starting to bounce a little on their own beds. I take a deep breath.

It seems like I've been standing here for an eternity—but it's probably been about seven seconds. Should I knock? Do I just walk in? Mom opens the door, saving me from the monkeys. She seems bigger than before. Not fatter or anything, but there's a calmness about her that makes her look bigger and stronger. She pulls me into her arms. Marcus comes running, yelling my name, and I hug him too.

Mom has cooked spaghetti and we sit down to eat. There's a vase of purple flowers in the middle of the table, and I think that I can ask what kind they are if we run out of things to talk about. Mom says she gets to bring home different arrangements from the florist shop and they make the whole house smell nice. It's a good smell, but I'm kind of missing the delicious soup aroma that's normally floating in the air. I don't say anything about that, though.

We talk about Mom's job and tomato sauce and Starscape Man and pigs in space and if they could survive or not—according to Marcus, they could as long as they had their little space-pig suits on. Mom and I laugh at the same time and I think we are both imagining Marcus's pigs in space wearing little space-pig suits.

After dinner, we watch a movie about a man, a dog, and a cat that trade places (or something like that), but the only part I pay attention to is when the man tries to drive but he's actually a dog, and the dog who's now a man jumps in the car. It's a little hard to focus, being at home, when it's not like home was before. I'm not waiting for Mom to walk in drunk or yell at us for being loud. I don't want that, but it's weird that things are different. It's weird, but I think it's good weird. I'm just not used to it yet. I'm home but it's not like being home, if that makes any sense at all.

Marcus really loved the movie but fell asleep before it ended. "I'm gonna put Marcus to bed," Mom says, and I notice that's different, too, but I just nod. "And then you and I could do some beading if you want." I nod again but I'm surprised. I've never seen Mom bead in my entire life. But I'm trying my best to go with this, this new good weirdness, so I don't say anything. I sit on the old green couch in the quiet, and the monkeys are there, moving around a little bit, but they're not bouncing off the walls. I think they're just letting me know they're not ready to sleep yet. I sink into a familiar groove in the couch and take in the newness of my home life.

Mom comes back with a container full of beads. She asks if there is anything specific I want to learn to bead. I tell her I'd like to bead some earrings for me and for Nohkum. She brings the lamp near us and switches it on. She puts the radio on low and soft music fills the room. She looks like she knows what she's doing, so I ask her how she learned to bead. She says, "All Indians know how to bead . . . ha, ha! Just kidding! I learned from Mechelle. She taught me a few things that I can teach you now." I laugh because Mom is pretty funny, just like her mom.

We listen to the music as we bead by lamplight and I thank her out of the blue. I don't think she's expecting that.

"For what?" she asks, as she puts her beading on the table. I keep working, looping each purple bead onto my needle.

"For loving us and for getting us back. I know Nohkum couldn't come back for you when you were a kid, and you could have just walked away..." Mom lets out a sob and I get up to hug her. She tells me that she wasn't sure if I would ever speak to her again. I cry in her arms as she apologizes to me, for almost losing me, for almost losing Marcus. I apologize to her for almost writing her off. This week I have cried so many tears. Grace says it's because now I feel safe enough to process everything that's happened.

I hear scratching at the back door and get up to open it. How could I have forgotten about Toofie? I scoop her into my arms and go back to the living room. "The cat came back, did she?" Mom goes to the kitchen and rummages through the cupboard. "Here, Toofie!" she calls as she shakes the kibble bag, and Toofie jumps out of my arms. Mom places the cat's bowl on the floor and Toofie digs in with gusto. "You know, this cat helped me out a lot when I was here alone. She slept with me, watched TV with me, and even ate with me. She's a good cat, Eva."

We make some tea, then go back to our beading. In this calm moment, I decide to ask Mom if I can interview her for my social studies assignment. She's not who I thought I'd be interviewing when I first got the assignment, but that seems like a hundred years ago now. I decided since I can't really interview anyone in my family about where they're originally from or how they got to Canada, I'm going to interview Mom about where she is now and how she got here. Mr. Harris is just going to have to deal with the fact that we're Native and we've always been here.

I tell Mom my assignment is to write about our family. What I don't tell her is that I'm only writing about one family member—her. The first question I ask is if there's one thing in the world she could change, what would it be.

She puts down her beading, sits back in her chair, and reaches for her tea, which is probably super cold now. She's deep in thought. She finally says, "There's a lot of things that have been hard, Eva, that maybe I could wish to change— like my mom leaving, or maybe me being in care, or maybe quitting drinking earlier." She stops. "But I wouldn't change a thing. Do you know why? Because we wouldn't be who we are today if a single thing was changed." I think about it—and I have to agree with her about that. "We wouldn't be here in this moment together," she says, as she picks up her beading again and smiles at me. I notice for the first time that she's wearing glasses. I ask her why, and she tells me aging just creeps up on you. One day no glasses, the next day she's borrowing Nohkum's reading glasses.

I ask Mom more questions about when she was a kid and a teenager. I find out a lot about her that I didn't know before. Finally, she takes off Nohkum's glasses and rubs her eyes. I ask her one final, important question, important to me any-way: what her favourite ice cream is. She says it is bananas Foster, which is bananas, vanilla ice cream, and caramel. She takes her mug into the kitchen, then comes back and kisses me on my forehead and says good night. I'm a little sad that she's going to bed, but I think we'll have other nights like this when I move back home. I tell her I love her, and she hugs me tight and says, "I love you more."

Before I go up to my room, I take the purple journal out of my backpack and set it on the kitchen table. I don't think I need it anymore, now that I'm actually getting to know my mom. I already know her better now.

Tonight, it's a little hard to sleep because the sounds of the creaking house are different than at Grace's and it's a bit colder. I go to the closet and grab one of Nohkum's sweaters and put it on. Toofie lies at the foot of my bed. My mind is busy, thinking of everything my mom told me tonight. But I'm not anxious now. The monkeys are asleep, and so I go to sleep too.

THE NEXT DAY I take my mom and Marcus for pizza with the twenty bucks Grace gave me. We order a large half-Hawaiian, half-cheese pizza, and it costs the same even without toppings on the one half, which I think is kind of a rip-off, but the Hawaiian side is so good that I can't be that mad about it.

Mike and Verna pick up Marcus first and he doesn't even cry. Mom had just told him he was going to come home soon. When Grace comes to get me, Mom and Grace stand on the front steps, talking about the best colleges and the best places to shop for cheap produce and clothes. Are they going to be friends? I hope so.

Grace and I drive back to the group home and when we walk through the door, I feel sad. I wanted to stay with my mom.

———————

I SPEND THAT NIGHT and most of the next morning in my room. Misty hasn't been back, so I have peace and quiet to work on my social studies assignment.

I think about everything my mom said when I interviewed her. There's a lot I wish I'd known a long time ago, but then I think about how everything that's happened has brought us here. I think and think. And then I write and write.

When I'm finished, I find Grace in the kitchen.

"Hi Eva," she says, gently, like she can tell how I'm feeling.

"I . . . can you read this? I mean, I wrote this and . . ."

She takes the paper from me and sits down at the table. I sit across from her, a bit uncomfortable. I don't usually show my writing to anyone, but for some reason, I needed to share this.

My Interview Assignment
By Nevaeh Brown

For this assignment, I decided to write about my family's history, but not my faraway, long-dead ancestors. I wanted to focus on the history that got us—me, my mom, my nohkum, and my little brother—here, right now, in our falling-down house in this middle-of-nowhere place called Hope.

So I decided to interview my mom about how she got here. Not here, like Canada or Hope, but here, like at this point in her life.

I learned that my mom's favourite ice cream is bananas Foster, which is basically bananas, caramel, and vanilla ice cream. I didn't know that until I asked her... just a couple of days ago. How does a daughter go through her entire life not knowing things about their own mother (especially if they live together)? This is a question I just recently started to ask myself.

When my mom was a little girl, she did not live with her mom, my nohkum, because she was taken away by child welfare. She did not see her mom again until she was an adult. My nohkum's history is part of our present, too. She went to residential school and it was horrible. Being there took away so much from her and when she left, she didn't know how to have good relationships. When she had my mom, she didn't know how to be a good parent.

It's hard for me to understand what it must have been like for my mom to grow up without a mom, because as mad as I have been at her, I still can't imagine my life without her. I can't imagine not seeing her face or hearing her tap her fingers on the table when she is deep in thought. I can't imagine not being able to tell her that I am sorry for being so angry at her for so long.

Not very long ago, my mom made some really big mistakes and my brother and I ended up in care. I was so angry at her. I was angry before that, but this made it way worse. But my mom surprised me. She tried to get us back. She fought for us. That showed me that she loves us with all her heart. She has made a lot of mistakes, but everyone makes mistakes. I don't know that I will forget those mistakes, but I think I can forgive her. I have made mistakes too and I hope she'll forgive me.

So in my family's history, we haven't always been together. My nohkum was alone at residential school without her family. And my mom was in care without her family, too. My brother and I were taken away and we were split apart. I can see that this isn't one person's fault or my family's fault. This is something much bigger than us.

My mom thought she was the worst mother in the world but she kept hanging on. She could have walked away from us, but something in her made her stay and that something is love. Love is part of my family's history too.

My mom's life hasn't been easy, but she is trying to move forward, for us. She deserves to be happy and to have bananas Foster every day. When I get older, that is one thing I can do for her: make sure she always has caramel in the cupboard, bananas in a bowl, and vanilla ice cream in the freezer.

Grace looks up at me and I'm surprised that she has tears in her eyes. Then I'm surprised that I have tears in my eyes too.

"Eva—I'm proud of you," she says. And I feel proud of myself too.

35

I Am the Champion!

ANOTHER WEEK PASSES and I'm just waiting. Waiting to be able to move home, waiting for Nohkum to get better, waiting for whatever life will look like from now on. I handed in my social studies assignment, visited Nohkum, hung out with Jared, avoided Mandy... but even while I was doing all that, I was still waiting.

When I get to school on Monday morning, I'm feeling sad thinking of my mom at home all alone. Marcus and I had another sleepover on Friday night and it was good weird again. Maybe not quite as weird as the first one. It's like I was prepared for it to be weird, so it wasn't so weird after all.

I dial Mom's number on my dinosaur phone. She picks up on the second ring.

"Mom, it's only me."

"Only you? It's not only you, it's the one and only you!" I laugh at her attempt at a joke. "Is everything okay?" she asks.

"Yeah. I just wanted to see how you and Toofie are."

"Toofie is lounging on the couch and I am looking at... well, I'm looking at colleges."

"Mom! That's awesome! You would do great in school!"

"You think so?" she asks, her voice softer when she is unsure.

"Of course! But I gotta go, I'm at school and I need to hide my dinosaur phone." Mom laughs.

I open the front doors and see Mr. Perry walking quickly toward me. He's moving even faster than usual.

"Nevaeh! I have the best news ever!" Mr. Perry looks like he's going to explode with happiness or pop like a balloon. Before I can say anything, he blurts out, "You won! 'Sweet-grass' won the poetry contest! I knew you could do it!"

"W-W-What? I won?"

"Yes!" Mr. Perry puts his hand up for a high five and I high five him, aware this is probably not the coolest thing to do—but who cares!

Mr. Perry hands me an envelope. I open it and inside is a cheque from *Medicine Wheel Magazine* for a thousand dollars. A thousand dollars! With my name on it! I am shaking. Does this mean I'm a writer?

"Nevaeh, I am so proud of you! See you in class!" Mr. Perry yells over his shoulder as he walks away, hurrying from a to b to c, probably on his way to help another lost kid. I'll never admit that I said this, but it's like he's some kind of angel in the world. He's helped me more than he'll ever know.

By the end of the school day, I've spent my thousand dollars a thousand different ways, but one thing I haven't changed my mind about is buying Nohkum a bed. I'm also thinking about buying my mom a new coat. The one she wears was once beautiful but is pilling and fading. I imagine her in a new coat that will keep her warm. And for Marcus? It's got to be Starscape Man sheets.

36

Closing Old Chapters

THE WEEK GOES by slowly until, finally, I find myself packing to go back home. The last few weeks have been a roller coaster. Misty hasn't come back and I wonder about where they are, if they're okay. As I pack, I notice a few of their things—a wooden zebra and lion sit on the dresser, and their "Relax Don't Do It" T-shirt hangs in the closet. I notice Grace watching me from the doorway and turn my head and smile.

"I think I'll just keep Misty's stuff like that for a while," she says. I nod.

Grace steps into the room and opens the drapes. "I can't wait for winter to be over. It won't be long now until spring pops its head in, bringing more light. You'll like that, hey Eva?"

It seems kind of weird that she's talking about basically nothing, but I don't say that. She seems a little sad. I nod again.

Rhys and Ty come in to give me a hug. Rhys gives me a novel by Lee Maracle called *Daughters Are Forever*. Ty tells me not to be a stranger and says he means it. He says my soup and bannock are the best he's ever had, and I tell him that my nohkum's are actually the best and one day I'll invite him and Rhys over for dinner, and I mean it.

When Rhys and Ty leave the room, Grace comes closer and looks me in the eyes. "Well. It looks like a nice day to go home, my dear." I see tears forming in Grace's eyes and give her a big hug.

"I've seen you come so far, Eva... so far, and I want you to know my door is always open, if and when you need me, even if it's just to come say hi. You got that?" I nod because I don't want to cry.

"Grace, I'm so thankful you came into my life when you did. You helped me so much. You were the absolute right place for me to land in the middle of my shit storm."

Grace pulls me in for another hug. "Okay, little lady, you better finish packing so I can drop you off at home. I bought Toofie a huge bag of cat food, and if you ever need more, just let me know." The thought of Grace buying the cat food for Toofie, for me, really makes me want to cry. Cat food! I shake my head. I've heard of crying over spilled milk, but not cat food!

Grace leaves the room and I continue packing. I take one of the sweaters Grace bought me and put it in Misty's drawer, along with my last chocolate bar. I think Misty will be back when they're ready. I know Grace will always have a soft spot for them. Misty kinda grows on everyone, like beautiful rainbow moss.

Jared knocks on the door frame and runs into the room. When he bounces onto the bottom bunk, it lets out a loud squeak.

"I hope that was fun!" I say.

He turns over on his side and rests his head on his hand. "Not really," he says with a fake-serious look on his face.

I throw a pillow at him. "You almost broke the bed, you nerd!"

Jared throws it back. "You're the nerd. Come on, give me a hug before you go." Jared stands up and we hug. It feels so nice, until he says, "It's getting warm in here... did you fart?" I push him away and laugh.

Grace calls me from down the hall. "Let's go, Eva, I told them I'd have you there early!"

Jared gives me another hug and whispers, "You got this, Eva. You ever need me, I'll be there."

"Isn't that an old song?" I raise my eyebrows at him and he groans.

"Why can't you just let me have this?"

I shake my head and give him a little shove out the door. We both laugh and I'm on my way.

37

A New Good Weird

'VE BEEN HOME for a week now, and for once, I'm not afraid of the future. I've even stopped waiting next door to hear if it's safe to go inside.

Mom stands in front of the sink peeling potatoes. We're making soup and bannock and we're going to bring some to the hospital for Nohkum. She'll be ready to come home in a few days and I can't wait. When she gets home, she'll see the new mattress I bought her. I got her a new T-shirt, too, that says, "Get off my way! Bingo's about to start!" I couldn't resist. I know she'll cry and I know she'll laugh, too.

Since I came home, Mom and I have made a pact. She says she doesn't plan on slipping but if she drinks again, she'll let me know, and I respect her for that. If she drinks and Nohkum can't take care of us, Marcus and I will go stay at Becka's place. I wish Mom could guarantee that won't happen, but I know guarantees aren't really possible in this life. The only guarantee is change. We just hope for the best and make plans for whatever might happen. It's good we've got a plan. And Marcus and I would be with people who care about us.

I finally pressed send on that email to Mel before I left Grace's. She emailed me back and congratulated me on winning the poetry contest. She didn't say she forgave me, but she did say it might be a good idea for me to use some of my money to buy her lunch one day, so I think that means she's going to try.

Mom says that if she drinks once Nohkum comes home, she'll stay away and come back when she's sober. I can't help it—the monkeys get going when I start to worry about where she'll stay and what might happen when she's gone and how long it will be before she comes back—but she says that's her problem. And I have to leave it at that. I had a good talk with Mechelle about how relapse is a part of recovery and it might be part of Mom's recovery too. And I think of the patience that Jared has had with his mom. Relapse is part of recovery. I get it now.

"Jared called for you while you were in the shower," Mom says as she dices the potatoes into bite-sized pieces.

"Oh, okay," I say, as I dig in the cupboard for the flour and baking powder.

"Is he cute?" Mom squeaks out and I look at her. She looks guilty of being friggin' weird.

"Oh my god, Mom, no... I mean, he's a friend... how would I know if he's cute or not?" I stammer out. Then *I* feel guilty of being friggin' weird. "I mean, you'll see him when he comes over." Jared is coming for dinner this Sunday.

Nohkum should be home by then and hopefully making her famous soup and bannock.

Mom laughs and I do too. Marcus comes in and asks if we're talking about him and Mom says, yes, we were talking about how cute he is. She winks at me and I toss a small handful of flour in her hair. Not sure why I did that, but I did. What does she do? She grabs a huge handful of flour and throws it at me. She laughs her head off when it lands with a poof on my face. Even my eyelashes are covered with flour! Who starts a flour fight for no reason? Me and my mom, that's who.

"I can't believe you did that!" I blurt out through my laughter as I grab a whole handful of flour and throw it back. I miss, and the flour hits Marcus in the face. I think he's going to cry and I think Mom does too, because we both stop. But Marcus just sits on the floor and laughs and laughs and says, "You look like a snowman!"

I guess we can't just flour-fight our way through life, as fun as it is. When we finally finish laughing and dusting ourselves off, we turn our focus back to the soup. Mom fries up a half-pound of hamburger with onions and garlic, drains it, and adds it to the pot. I help her dice the carrots and Marcus stands on a chair in front of the sink washing the dishes, or at least his version of it, washing only the front side of anything made of plastic.

He seems older now. He doesn't come to me when he gets hurt anymore—he goes to Mom. At first that made me sad, but it made me sadder to think of how he should have been going to her in the first place. He's building a relationship with her and that's good. And so am I.

Mom adds a whole can of crushed tomatoes to the soup, plus corn, macaroni, and salt and pepper. Nohkum's soup pot boils with fury, making the gurgling sound that's always so comforting.

I make the bannock like Nohkum showed me and Mom comes over to help. I look at her and she's watching me. She looks happy. She boops my nose with her floury hands and I say, "Come on now, don't start what you can't finish!" Mom laughs.

Suddenly, I feel it. I notice that the monkeys are still, like not even moving a tiny bit. When did that happen? I know they'll be back—Nohkum says they always come back—but now that I know what makes them go nuts, I can get them back into their cages a bit faster. I imagine the monkeys lying there on crisp, white sheets, sound asleep and dreaming.

I'm so happy to be home. The days look brighter now. I couldn't have imagined this a few months ago, a few weeks ago—making a family dinner with my mom, looking forward to what might happen next. It's all so weird, where we are now and how we ended up here. It's a new good weird.

Acknowledgments

'D LIKE TO acknowledge the support of grants from the University of British Columbia for research and everyone in the Creative Writing Department (Bronwen Tate, Sheryda Warrener, Linda Svendsen, Stephen Hunt, Kevin Chong, Carol Shaben, Alix Ohlin, Tanya Kyi, Doretta Lau, Maureen Medved, and the late Bryan Wade) for everything you have taught me. I'd also like to acknowledge Alison Acheson, the first professor to read the first chapter of this book, who saw a grain of sand, enough to grow a pearl. I'd like to acknowledge the love and support of the wonderful people at HighWater Press, including Caley Clements (editor extraordinaire) for being on this journey with me, Nevaeh, and Toofie; Catherine Gerbasi for being such a supporter of my work and research; Irene Velentzas; Kirsten Phillips; and all the others working behind the scenes. Thank you to

Jason Lin, for the amazing cover art. I'd also like to acknowledge Victor John, who always had my back in my education and writing endeavours, and Kehewin Cree Nation, which continues to push forward in trying to pave the road for a brighter future for upcoming generations. And thank you to Grace Woo, for gluing yourself to my family when we needed you! Last but not least, thank you to the Social Sciences and Humanities Research Council and the Aboriginal Graduate Fellowship for financial support during my MFA. I appreciate you all.

WANDA JOHN-KEHEWIN (she, her, hers) is a Cree writer who uses her work to understand and respond to the near destruction of First Nations cultures, languages, and traditions. When she first arrived in Vancouver on a Greyhound bus, she was a pregnant nineteen-year-old carrying little more than a bag of chips, a bottle of pop, thirty dollars, and hope. After many years travelling (well, mostly stumbling) along her healing journey, Wanda brings her personal experiences to share with others. Now a published poet and fiction author, she writes to stand in her truth and to share that truth openly. Wanda is the mother of five children, one dog, two cats, and one angelfish, and grandmother to one super-cute granddog. She calls Coquitlam home until the summertime, when she treks to the Alberta prairies to visit family and learn more about Cree culture and tradition.

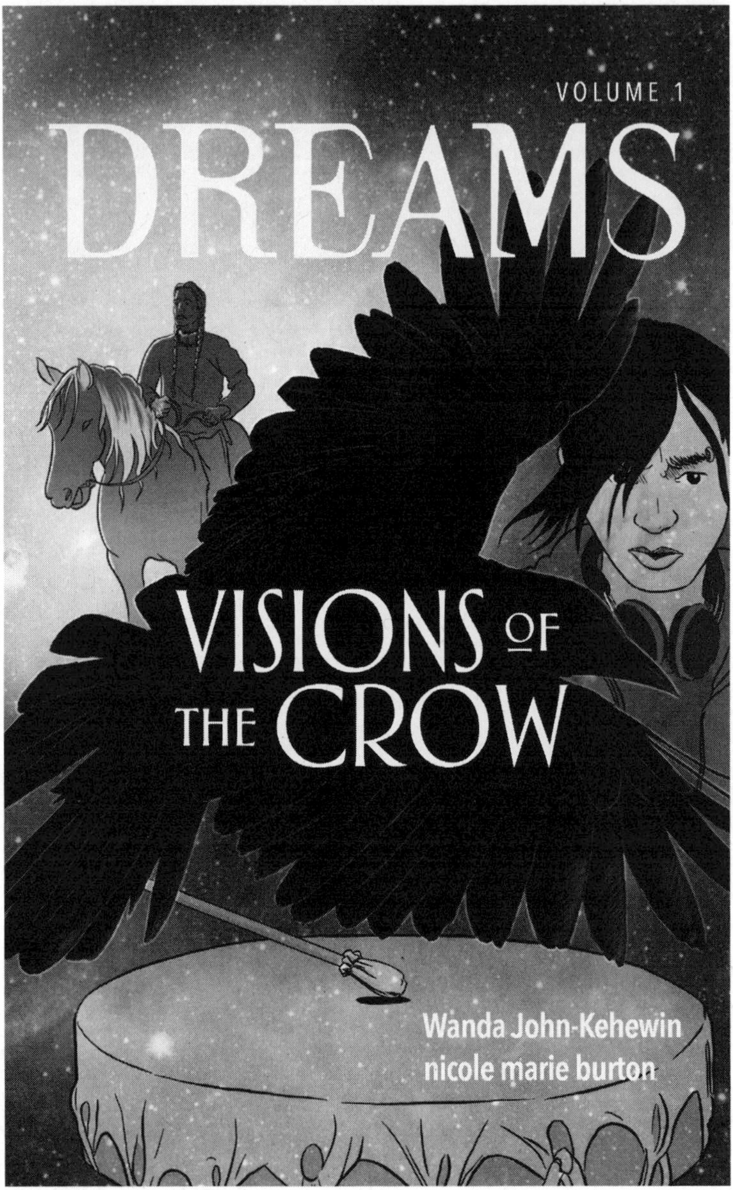
VOLUME 1
DREAMS
VISIONS OF THE CROW
Wanda John-Kehewin
nicole marie burton

Also from Wanda John-Kehewin,
the graphic novel series,

DREAMS

Damon Quinn is just trying to survive high school:
get to class on time, avoid the school bully, lie
low. Everything changes when Damon begins to
have waking dreams where the past collides with
the present. Will these dreams be disastrous for
Damon or the beginning of a new adventure?

Scan the QR code
to find out more
about Damon's story.